JESSICA COLE

MODEL SPY

D0541983

JESSICA COLE
MODEL SPY
CODE RED LIPSTICK

SARAH SKY

SCHOLASTIC

First published in the UK in 2014 by Scholastic Children's Books
An imprint of Scholastic Ltd
Euston House, 24 Eversholt Street
London, NW1 1DB, UK
Registered office: Westfield Road, Southam, Warwickshire, CV47 0RA
SCHOLASTIC and associated logos are trademarks and/or registered
trademarks of Scholastic Inc.

ISBN 978 1407 14017 9

A CIP catalogue record for this book
is available from the British Library.

Printed by CPI Group (UK) Ltd, Croydon, CR0 4YY
Papers used by Scholastic Children's Books are made
from wood grown in sustainable forests.

1 3 5 7 9 10 8 6 4 2

www.scholastic.co.uk/zone

For Darren, James and Luke

CHAPTER ONE

The giant snake squeezed her neck and dragged her deeper beneath the surface of the icy water. Jessica felt weak from the cold, and her shoulders ached beneath the snake's enormous weight. Her lungs were beginning to get tight. She tried to pull the snake off but it was longer than her from head to toe and impossible to budge.

Panic gripped her as she dropped to the bottom of the tank. She had cramps in both legs. Her limbs felt like lead weights. She tried to kick her way up but nothing happened. She could see blurred figures on the other side of the glass but nobody came to her rescue. They were going to watch her drown. She felt so stupid. Her dad had warned her it was a bad idea.

1

She hated it when he was right, which was pretty much *all* the time. Why hadn't she listened to him?

Her lungs screamed for oxygen and her ribs felt like they were cracking one by one. She wasn't going to die like this, not in front of these people. With one final burst of energy, she yanked at the snake. The sudden movement took it by surprise and it slid off her shoulders, momentarily beaten. She feebly kicked to the surface, concentrating on the circle of light. She broke through the water and clung on to the side of the tank, taking huge gulps of air as figures lunged towards her.

"Hair! Lipstick and eyeliner!" a voice boomed. "And will somebody grab that snake?"

Jessica shivered violently as a group of make-up artists applied more silver waterproof eyeshadow, black eyeliner and mascara. A stylist combed her hair and smothered it with gel while another pair of hands readjusted the green chiffon kaftan over her white Gucci swimsuit and pinned it back into place. She looked down at her fingers, which had actually turned blue. Wasn't anybody going to ask her if she was OK? They were clearly too busy trying to make her look as flawless as possible before they tried to drown her again.

A small man carrying a shih-tzu strode towards her. His tiny black beard quivered with anger.

"Jessica, *tu es très belle*, but how many times have I asked you not to blink? Why were you kicking about when I specifically told you to float? You've ruined my shot. Again!"

She resisted the urge to reach out and drag him into the water along with his horrible yappy dog. He was, after all, Sebastian Rossini. He'd hand-picked her to feature in a spread in *Mademoiselle*, the new glossy magazine for teenagers. It was a great opportunity. She was thrilled. Unfortunately, he also happened to be a total sadist. There was no point arguing with him; he wouldn't let her go until he got the shot he wanted.

"I'm s-s-sorry," she said, teeth chattering. "I lost my concentration for a moment. It won't happen again, I p-p-promise."

"*C'est bon.*"

He shoved his dog into his assistant Juan's trembling hands and picked up his camera again. Juan put the dog down on a Chanel cushion in the corner of the warehouse and pushed a snack of poached chicken in front of him before backing off to a safe distance. Jessica's stomach rumbled. She'd been here since the crack of dawn and hadn't been offered any breakfast or a drink. Why did everyone think modelling was glamorous? If only some of the girls at school could see her now. They'd soon shut up.

She flexed her arms and legs. The circulation was coming back. Just.

"Hold still and open your lips wider," a make-up artist ordered.

She obeyed as a third coat of scarlet lipstick was applied and blotted with a tissue. Somebody else touched up her waterproof foundation.

"Again!" Sebastian said. "And no mistakes this time."

"I'll try!"

She smiled brightly despite wanting to tell him to drop dead. Two men had fished the snake out of the tank and gently placed it back on to her shoulders. She took a deep breath and sank below the surface again. This time she kept her eyes wide open despite the water stinging like mad. She struck a pose, arched her back and let her arms drift up to her shoulders. She changed position again. Her legs floated gracefully behind her. It was hard to hold her body and juggle the snake, but ballet and kick-boxing classes had helped build up her stamina. She was determined to give Sebastian the perfect shot so she could get out of there ASAP.

She struck a final pose and Sebastian gave a thumbs-up. It was a wrap. She broke through the water for the last time and was greeted with a round of applause from the shoot team. She shrugged the snake off her shoulders with a shudder, and felt herself being pulled out of the tank. She was so cold she could barely walk down the ladder, but so what? She should quit griping and suck it up; it was a great job. She got to meet some amazingly creative people. Plus, hopefully she'd have the chance to travel around the world on assignments soon. This job would give her an awesome shot for her portfolio, and that could lead to something bigger. She'd love to land an ad campaign for a cosmetics company or a fashion label like Prada.

"*Fantastique! Ma jolie sirène,*" Sebastian said, beaming.

She blushed, almost wishing she hadn't been able

to translate "my beautiful mermaid" – embarrassing or what?

"T-t-thank you," she said, stuttering with cold.

She limped away to a changing room. She'd made it out alive. Louise greeted her with a sympathetic smile and a large white towel.

"You'll soon warm up, I promise," she said. "Now let's get you out of this wet stuff."

Louise had to pull off the kaftan and swimsuit, as Jessica's fingers were too numb. Hugging the towel to her, she shrugged on a pink bathrobe. This shoot was better than most, as it had a separate changing area, but photographers and stylists often barged in unannounced. Other models didn't bat an eyelid about dressing and undressing in front of everyone on a shoot, but she still hadn't got used to it. She doubted she would.

Peeling off her false eyelashes and scrubbing at the make-up with cotton-wool balls, she slowly began to recognize herself through the layers of foundation. She didn't wear heavy make-up like this when she wasn't working, although she *was* surgically attached to her favourite lipgloss and mascara.

Louise teased the gel and wax out of her long strawberry-blonde hair before starting blow-drying as Jessica checked her mobile. That was a first. Her dad hadn't texted. He usually suffered from OSDS – Overprotective Single Dad Syndrome – and wanted her to check in with him as soon as a shoot finished. He was away on business and hadn't returned her calls from yesterday either; they'd gone straight to voicemail. Maybe he was just busy. Was that the reason why she hadn't found a text from Jamie, the hottest boy in her year, either?

Yeah, right. In her dreams. Like he'd ever message her.

"You could do with a shampoo," Louise exclaimed. "I'm never going to get these knots out." She lifted up a clump of tangled hair.

"Don't worry," Jessica replied, scraping her hair into an untidy bun. A few tendrils refused to be coaxed back into place but she didn't have time to tame them. It was 7.45 a.m. already and she was stuck in east London, nowhere near a tube station. Her teachers had been pretty accommodating since she'd started modelling but she didn't want to push her luck by turning up late for registration again. One more strike and she'd be heading straight to detention.

After wriggling into her regulation grey polyester skirt, white shirt and grey pullover, she stepped into black ballet pumps. She hardly ever wore heels as she was so tall. She sighed as she stared into the mirror. It didn't matter how many times she tugged at her skirt, it didn't look any better. Yeuch! The fabric scratched and edged up her legs. It drew way too much attention to the fact her legs looked like they belonged to a giraffe.

She fastened her mum's gold pendant and tucked it beneath her blouse so it wouldn't be confiscated, then threw on the grey, ruffled pea coat she'd found in a vintage clothes market. It had *just* scraped through the strict uniform rules. She'd almost made it out of the door when Sebastian burst in, brandishing his digital camera. His dog yapped around his heels.

"We have the shot, *ma jolie sirène*. Look at this."

Jessica and Louise peered over his shoulder at the photograph. A beautiful sylphlike girl floated in the water as naturally as if she'd been born there. Her blonde tresses streamed behind her and a mysterious smile lingered on her lips. She barely recognized herself – she really *had* been transformed into a mermaid. Nobody would ever guess she'd almost drowned.

"Blimey!" Louise said. "That looks nothing like you. You scrub up well, if you don't mind me saying. I wouldn't know it was you."

Jessica blushed.

"Well, I didn't mean that exactly," Louise said. "It's just that you look so different."

"I know what you mean," Jessica said. "It doesn't feel like me when I'm modelling."

Sebastian nodded. "That's the quality of great models. They can transform themselves with the help of an artist like me. You're a blank canvas that can become anything, Jessica, including a mermaid."

She flinched as he kissed her on both cheeks and disappeared with a dramatic flourish.

"I didn't mean to be rude." Louise turned towards her, frowning.

"I know. Don't worry about it."

Jessica gave her a hug and hurried away. Louise lacked in the tact department, but still, she much preferred assistants who spoke their minds rather than the ones who made catty comments about her appearance behind her back. Jessica was the first to admit she didn't look like the Cindy Crawfords or Claudia Schiffers who used to dominate the modelling world with their curvy figures and perfectly balanced features. Jessica's forehead was a little broad and her jaw stronger than most girls her age, accentuating her large green eyes and the freckles on her upturned nose.

Shouting her goodbyes to the rest of the shoot team, she strode through the warehouse. Jessica closed the door behind her and smiled as she felt the winter sun warm her face. Without make-up on she looked like any other teenage girl.

It felt good, apart from the horrid uniform. Even the world's most famous supermodel couldn't pull this look off. She gave the skirt one last tug and sprinted for the bus.

CHAPTER
TWO

Jessica was wedged under a middle-aged man's armpit while the driver attempted to reach kamikaze speeds in Monday rush-hour traffic. Great. Yet another journey stuck next to someone with bad B.O. Slowly, she turned around to find today's newspaper shoved in her face, and couldn't help but read the story.

January 20

TYLER QUITS!
Supermodel Tyler Massey has shocked the fashion world by turning her back on her lucrative modelling career.

The eighteen-year-old unexpectedly quit her

multimillion-pound contract with Naturissmo SkinCare Company yesterday and cancelled all her fashion commitments, including her first solo front cover of Vogue.

She'd already pulled out of a much-anticipated appearance at Paris Haute Couture Week this Thursday and hasn't been seen in public since before Christmas.

Her publicist said plans to launch her own perfume have also been put on hold indefinitely.

Lydia Hollings, boss of Emerald modelling agency, says Tyler wants to enrol at college. However, her whereabouts are currently unknown and she has not returned to her hometown in Devon.

Tyler is the last of the "famous five" supermodels to quit the fashion industry.

Olinka, Jacey, Darice and Valeriya have all left modelling in the last month, citing personal reasons. They have now retired from public life.

The "famous five" phrase was coined by Sebastian Rossini, who photographed the supermodels for a legendary Vogue front cover.

Jessica looked away as the woman turned the page. She'd heard of the "famous five". Who hadn't? They were all well-known enough to be referred to by just their first names. Why were they all leaving the business? The bus suddenly braked, jolting everyone forward. The doors clattered open and a stream of people staggered off.

She clung on to the handrail and swung down into an empty seat. Digging around in her black rucksack, she pulled out her iPhone and typed the name "Tyler" and "supermodel" into the search engine. It brought up thousands of hits. The internet was buzzing with rumours about why she'd retired from modelling. They varied from her being disfigured in a car crash to falling victim to alien abduction.

Seriously? Did anyone actually believe that?

She followed links about the rest of the "famous five". Olinka had been due to start shooting a major Hollywood movie when Lydia Hollings unexpectedly announced her retirement earlier this month. Jacey had been planning to launch her own exclusive lingerie line and perfume. Emerald had landed bookings for Darice and Valeriya from practically every top designer at Paris Haute Couture Week. They'd both recently pulled out despite being the stars of the shows. Emerald again. She clicked back. Jacey was also an Emerald model. The supermodels belonged to the same agency and they'd all walked away from exciting jobs at the peak of their careers. How strange.

She typed in the names of all the supermodels, Lydia Hollings and Emerald. She found an article from *OK!* magazine dated last December.

THE FAMOUS FIVE DAZZLE EVERYONE –
AGAIN!

No one could be accused of being underdressed at Emerald modelling agency's fiftieth anniversary ball in London.

The "famous five" pulled out all the stops, wearing £20 million worth of emeralds and diamonds between them, loaned by De Beers.

They rubbed glamorous shoulders with designers, magazine editors and other celebrities, including Hollywood stars Taylor Lautner and Liam Hemsworth.

Guests paid tribute to Lydia Hollings, the head of Emerald, who has made the modelling agency the most successful in the world. She famously scouted Tyler, Olinka, Jacey, Darice and Valeriya.

Happy birthday, Emerald!

Lydia Hollings was in the centre of the photograph. Jessica enlarged the screen. What a trout pout! It was hilarious. She'd obviously had too much collagen pumped into her lips. That was Tyler, to her left, in a gorgeous ink-blue gown. The caption said it was Christian Dior. Olinka, Jacey, Darice and Valeriya were grouped around them, clutching champagne glasses and laughing. The girls all looked stunning, particularly Darice, who wore a scarlet-fringed Versace number slashed to her navel.

Why couldn't she find any more photos of the supermodels in public after the anniversary ball? After years of being in the public spotlight, they'd simply slipped away. Had they finally had enough of being followed by the paps? It had to grate, but it still didn't seem a good enough reason to give up. Tyler had years of modelling ahead of her and could have juggled her A levels with work. That was certainly what she was planning to do. The extra cash was pretty handy, particularly when her dad wasn't up to working.

Looking up, the familiar streets of west London whizzed past.

"No!" She hammered on the stop button, but the driver ignored her and whizzed through a red light. She should have got off two stops ago. It was 8.55 a.m. and she was seriously late. This was the third time a shoot had overrun in the last month. What excuse could she give this time?

A bad-tempered snake tried to drown me? Hatchet Hatcham would never buy it. She'd get a detention and a note sent home, which meant Dad would ground her, like, for ever. She'd made a pact with him that modelling wouldn't get in the way of schoolwork.

As soon as the doors swung open again, she dashed down the street, past cafés, launderettes and takeaways, not slowing until she reached St Alban's Comp. She clung on to the railings, panting. She'd just given Usain Bolt a run for his money. The front gates were open so she could still make it. She hesitated.

Form prefects would be lurking about, waiting to pounce on stragglers with their dreaded "late notes".

If she just charged in, detention would be a dead cert. She pulled out her dad's iPad from her rucksack and shoved in a headset. She turned the device on, waited for it to load and entered his secret password.

Jellybean.

Honestly. Her dad was a private detective and ex-MI6 agent. Couldn't he think of something less obvious – and hackable – than his old nickname for her?

Jessica bean – Jellybean.

She took a photograph of the school using the iPad and uploaded it on to the thermal heat-sensor application. Within seconds, she had a 3D image of the school and a seething mass of orange blobs which represented the pupils and staff inside. She didn't need every floor. She isolated the grounds, the route to the rear entrance and the whole of the ground floor just to be on the safe side, just as she'd done at a hotel in West Kensington when her dad needed her to help plant a bugging device in a target's suite.

She clicked on to "start audio" and gripped the iPad

tightly. Time to play. The screen showed two orange blobs walking along the perimeter of the building: patrolling form prefects.

"Enemy approaching from east in approximately thirty seconds," the electronic voice in her headset said. "Take a sharp left. Go now. Thirty, twenty-nine, twenty-eight, twenty-seven. . ."

Jessica tore through the gates into the deserted courtyard. She'd almost made it to the rear door.

"Stop!"

Jessica slammed against the wall, heart pounding

"Enemy passing. Five, four, three, two, one," the voice said.

Two prefects walked towards the bicycle sheds. As soon as their backs were turned, she flung open the door and burst into the corridor. She took a deep breath, awaiting instructions.

"Head north along corridor, two hundred metres. Stationary figures ahead. Caution advised."

She turned the corner, pressing herself against the wall as she moved slowly up the corridor. Up ahead, two boys were arguing. She reached the row of lockers and crouched behind them. Damnit. Tommy Williams, a prefect and world-class bully, blocked her escape route. No way could she talk her way round him. He'd take great delight in giving her a late note.

The instruction came. "Take corridor to left. Clear route to destination. Five, four, three, two, one."

Jessica stared at the screen. The monitors were retreating, probably back to their own classes. She hesitated. Tommy's braces glinted menacingly as he pinned a much smaller boy against the locker. He was rifling through his pockets, snatching coins.

She flicked off the thermal imaging programme and clicked on to "magnetization". She'd never tried this function before but it looked pretty cool. She scanned in Tommy's face and highlighted his enormous metal braces. He really did resemble a henchman in a James Bond movie.

"Let's see how you like this, Jaws."

Click.

"What the. . . ?" Tommy began.

A coin flew out of his fist and stuck to his braces.

Interesting. Using the mouse, she turned up the magnetization strength. More coins shot into the air and clamped to his mouth.

"Aargh!" Tommy screamed, clutching his face. The rest of his words were incomprehensible as he picked up the smaller boy by the lapels and threw him against the locker, mumbling something threatening.

"It's nothing to do with me," the boy protested.

As Tommy curled his fist into a punch, Jessica increased the magnetization. It tore him away from his victim and slammed him into the metal locker, mouth first. He tried to pull himself off but his braces were firmly stuck.

"Help!" His voice was muffled.

The boy seized his opportunity to escape and pegged it down the corridor. Jessica clicked the "off" button and Tommy slumped to the floor in a shower of coins. She didn't have time to gloat. She took off down the corridor to her left and burst through the door just as her form teacher snapped shut the red registration book.

Uh-oh.

"Late again, Miss Cole." A smirk spread across Mr Hatcham's face. "We're so honoured you deigned to pay us a visit instead of gracing a catwalk."

Now all eyes in class were on her. This was *so*

embarrassing. Becky flashed a sympathetic smile. Out of the corner of her eye, she could see a blond boy watching. Jamie. A hot red flush stole across her cheeks.

Mr Hatcham folded his arms over his large stomach. A couple of shirt buttons gave up the struggle to keep his belly inside and popped open. He was enjoying this. He always made digs about her modelling in the hope of making himself more popular with the other kids. *As if*.

"Perhaps one of these days you'll find the time to teach *me* a few things," he continued.

He jumped to his feet and attempted to strike a modelling pose, putting his hand behind his ear and pulling a silly face. A few girls tittered. Didn't he realize they were laughing at him, not her? She really did hate him. If only she could throw him into that tank with the snake!

"I'm sorry," she said through gritted teeth. "I can explain."

"I'm sure you can, Miss Cole," he said, raising an eyebrow. "You can explain at your leisure during detention with me tonight. We also have the pleasure of Jamie, who is equally incapable of turning up on time."

Jessica's heart did a somersault at the sound of Jamie's name, the way it always did. Now it was pounding faster. Did he realize the effect he had on her? His mouth widened into a smile, revealing perfect white teeth. He scraped his chair back and stood up. He was one of the few boys in the year group who was taller than her. He also had a seriously good body from all the sport he played. His shirt stretched impressively over his biceps.

"The pleasure's all mine." He took a deep bow and grinned at Jessica.

She blushed deep crimson as the class clapped and wolf-whistled.

"That's enough. Quiet, everyone!" Mr Hatcham snapped. "Sit down, Jessica. You've caused enough disruption for one morning. Becky, take those ridiculous earrings out or you'll be joining Jessica and Jamie at detention. And remember, no one likes being a gooseberry."

Jessica dived for her seat, next to her friend. She couldn't bring herself to meet Jamie's gaze as she sat down; she was red enough. Why was it she managed to stay calm whenever she accompanied her dad on covert assignments but when it came to Jamie she turned into a total wreck?

She looked across as her friend tucked her neat black bob behind her ears and pulled out a pair of dangly skull-and-crossbones.

"Bad journey?" Becky whispered.

Jessica sighed. "Same as ever."

CHAPTER THREE

"So you've finally landed a date with Jamie," Becky said through a mouthful of sandwich. "Congrats!"

She elbowed Jessica, who shuffled further along the bench. They always went to the local park for lunch, even in the winter, to escape from the claustrophobic classrooms and raucous younger pupils.

"It's hardly a date," Jessica said. "It's detention."

"But you'll be alone with him. Anything could happen. . ." Resting her head on Jessica's shoulder, she made smooching sounds.

"You're mad!" She shoved her friend off the bench with a laugh. "It's detention with Hatchet Hatcham, not dinner and a movie."

"Still. He might need to leave the room for a minute

and yours and Jamie's eyes could meet across Room 4B. . ."

"Very funny." She extended a hand to haul her back up again. "I mean, Jamie does have nice eyes and he's super-smart and everything. He really makes me laugh too."

"Don't forget he's got a super-hot body."

"Has he? I hadn't noticed."

They both erupted into giggles.

Jessica rummaged in her rucksack and pulled out her compact and a lipgloss. She clicked open the silver case.

"Oooh, let me guess what that does," Becky said. "The compact is really a tracking device so we can find Jamie right now and the lipgloss is a bug. We'll be able to listen to him talking about you to his mates."

Jessica rolled her eyes. "You've been watching way too many spy movies. I hate to disappoint you, but the compact is actually, er, a compact, and this is a lipgloss." She tapped Becky on the forehead with the tube before applying a peach slick to her lips.

"Not everything in here's a gadget," she said. "Just the iPad."

"If you say so!"

Jessica groped inside her rucksack and groaned. "I don't believe it."

"What is it?"

"I've forgotten *Jane Eyre*. I need it for English, last period."

"You've got time to get it, if you go now. I can cover for you with Hatchet Hatcham if you're a bit late for registration."

Jessica hugged her and ran off. She really could try out for the next Olympics with all the sprint training she'd been doing today. She passed Ealing Studios. Usually she tried to spot anyone famous lurking about; she and Becky had even got Robert Pattinson's autograph when he was shooting a period drama. But she didn't have time to wait around for heart-throbs today. She had to get home.

She didn't stop running until she reached the corner of Chislett Street, then half-walked, half-jogged past the tall Victorian houses. They all had large sash windows and stained glass above solid oak doors. Her house, number 67, was different in one obvious respect. Beside the front door was a small gold plaque with the words: *Jack Cole Private Investigations*. Visitors often missed the discreet sign. The other unique features of the house were even less conspicuous to the naked eye: the glass in all the windows was bulletproof, and above the ledges were slats which enabled steel shutters to roll down in an emergency.

Jessica let herself in with her key and paused. That was odd. The burglar alarm hadn't activated. A yellow light flashed on the box, indicating a fault. Her dad wouldn't like that one little bit. He was ultra security conscious after working for MI6 for twenty years. He'd retired early nine years ago after developing multiple sclerosis. That was when he'd set up his own private investigations agency, insisting he had no intention of sitting around waiting for the day when he'd end up in a wheelchair.

Jessica tapped the digits on the box to reset the alarm. A screeching noise blared out. She turned it off again. It was working now. Mattie had probably fiddled with it. Her grandma was staying over and slowly driving her nuts while Dad was away on a job all week. Mattie couldn't get her head round the DVD player, let alone any of her dad's high-tech security equipment. She was a total technophobe.

Jessica looked up. The CCTV camera had also malfunctioned. Maybe there'd been a power cut this afternoon. She dropped her rucksack on the floor and headed upstairs for her book; it was definitely by the side of her bed. She stopped. The study door was ajar, but it had been locked when she'd left this morning. Had Mattie broken the golden rule and gone in? Doubtful. She'd never dare. Jessica walked closer.

The first rule of surveillance her dad had ever drilled into her was to always take in her surroundings. Those were definitely scratch marks on the lock. The study door had been tampered with. Jessica glanced back at the burglar alarm. Someone had disabled the alarm and CCTV camera before picking open the door.

When she peeped inside, she saw that the room was tidy and ordered; a photo of her late mum from her modelling heyday was still in pride of place on the Thai oak desk. Dad's computer was still there. Jessica did a quick circuit of the ground floor; nothing seemed to have been taken. The stack of notes her dad had left still sat on the kitchen table. Surely a burglar would have snatched that booty? It was close to three hundred pounds – an easy hit for an opportunistic intruder.

Back in the hallway, she stared at the study. It was the only room that had been targeted, which was *really* bad news. Had the intruder discovered the house's biggest secret, the one that not even Mattie knew about? She had to check. It's what her dad would do if *he* were here now.

A creak startled her as she walked into the study. Someone was behind the door. Before she had time to turn around, an arm was around her chest and a cloth smothered her nose and mouth. A sweet, sickly scent filled her nostrils. She tugged at the gloved hand but her strength was gone. She felt weak and helpless, like a floppy rag doll. Why couldn't she move? She should try to kick or throw her head back to knock her attacker off guard, as she'd been taught in kick-boxing, but her limbs wouldn't obey her. Her head throbbed and her knees had given way. The painting on the wall spun round and round and the floorboards leapt up towards her. Then everything went black.

*

A sharp pain stabbed Jessica's forehead as she tried to open her eyes. The light seared her eyeballs and nausea gripped her. She fought the urge to throw up. She had to think. The intruder had been here the whole time and knocked her out. Probably with chloroform. Jessica opened her eyes, slowly this time. The study ceiling came into focus. She tried moving each arm and leg, one by one. Phew. She wasn't seriously hurt. She sat up, making her head spin.

Whoa! That was too quick. Sticking her head between her knees made her feel a lot less woozy. Jessica checked her watch. It had only been a matter of minutes, but the intruder would be long gone. Whoever had got in was a pro – bypassing Dad's high-tech burglar alarm and coming equipped with gloves and chloroform. Not your average burglar. But what were they looking for?

Jessica stared at the bookshelf, her hand hovering over the mobile phone in her blazer pocket. Should she call the police? No. Her dad might not want them involved. He'd probably call an old contact from MI6, given his security-services background and the fact this obviously wasn't a normal burglary.

It took a few minutes before she felt able to stand up. She steadied herself against the desk. When that felt OK, she focused on the bookshelves and walked straight ahead. Charles Darwin's *The Origin of Species* was centre right. She reached out for the large hardback book but it was already tipped forward. The bookcase had moved a fraction of an inch.

Someone *did* know the house's secrets and had opened her dad's hidden door. Jessica took a deep breath and pulled the bookcase wide open.

CHAPTER

FOUR

Cold, stale air filled Jessica's nostrils as she pulled the door behind her and stepped into the lift. She pressed the button to her left and crouched down; her legs still felt like jelly. The lift jolted as it descended to the basement. Once it stopped, she heaved open the grille.

Becky would never believe Jessica if she told her about the bunker. The walls and ceilings were lined with titanium-aluminium alloy, which was bullet- and bombproof. The house could come under mortar attack but it'd still be safe down here. Her dad even stored enough food and water for a week.

She flicked a switch and a computer suite was flooded with light. She looked about. This wasn't how she'd left it last night. She'd made sure everything was exactly as she'd found it when she'd borrowed the iPad; Dad would kill her if he thought she was using his equipment unsupervised. Files marked "MI6 confidential" were strewn over the floor. She knelt down and flicked one open. It contained the names of MI6 agents in Algeria. Another file listed French agents and a third was marked "Vectra". It contained a grainy photo of a dark-haired man, wearing sunglasses.

She pulled out her mobile and quickly rang her dad but it went straight to voicemail again.

Now what should she do?

This was seriously freaking bad news. The intruder must have been looking for MI6 agents, but what was Dad doing with their files after all this time anyway? They were dated this year. She looked around the room. On the right-hand side were the cupboards where he kept his equipment from his MI6 days, along with new purchases she secretly borrowed whenever he was away. She pulled open the drawers containing pens, key rings and hand-held games consoles – all hiding surveillance bugs. They were untouched, together with the equipment for picking locks and bugging phones. The intruder wasn't interested in a stack of fake driving licences and passports either.

Jessica stared at the ranks of computers and television screens. Her dad used the computer on the far side for monitoring tracking devices. It could trace where a person was anywhere in the world. A second computer identified and sifted through voice patterns. It was so sophisticated, it could get rid of all the background noise in a busy bar and pick up the words of a target who was whispering something in someone's ear. Both computers were turned off. She checked the CCTV equipment. Interior and exterior shots for the last month had been totally erased. The intruder hadn't taken any chances.

She flopped down in the chair in front of her dad's main computer. This was bad. *Really, really* bad. A green light flickered on the side of the black screen. It was already switched on. She tapped the keyboard and her dad's files appeared, scrolling down the screen. Whoever had broken in was an exceptionally good hacker. Dad never took chances with his work computer, unlike his iPad. Even she didn't know how to get in. It was protected with a series of encrypted passwords, but the intruder had still managed to access his secret files.

She flicked through the open documents. They were all about someone called Sam Bishop. One was a photo file containing pictures of a man in his thirties. He had bright blue eyes and dark hair. He appeared to be staring into direct sunlight, his hand shielding his right eye. In another, he was standing with his arm thrown around a grey-haired woman's shoulder.

She clicked open a letter her dad had scanned into the computer. It was from Mrs Bishop, of 33 Crabtree Gardens, Hastings, dated 6th January. It read:

Dear Mr Cole
I have given much consideration to our
telephone conversation and decided that I do
wish to employ you to find Sam. My fears for
his safety grow by the day and I feel I have
nowhere left to turn.

As we discussed, Sam was sacked from
Allegra Knight Skincare Company, based in
Paris, last October after he allegedly failed
a random drug test. He was also accused of

35

stealing items from the company. The French police believe he's gone on the run in Europe to escape prosecution, as he's made no attempt to re-enter the United Kingdom or get in touch with friends and family.

I refuse to believe this explanation and remain convinced the French police are involved in a cover-up. My son has been anti-drugs since he saw the impact of cannabis use on a few of his former school friends. I do not believe he is taking drugs.

I admit he seemed unhappy the last time we spoke. He wouldn't tell me what was bothering him but did talk about returning to Cambridge University soon to continue his research.

The company has been in touch to offer its support and to invite me to visit their offices in Paris, but my ill health prevents me from taking up its offer. I would be very grateful if you could visit on my behalf and investigate his disappearance.

Yours sincerely

Louisa Bishop

The final document was a copy of a small local newspaper cutting, dated last November.

MISSING SCIENTIST SPARKS POLICE PROBE

French police are investigating the disappearance of British scientist Sam Bishop, it was revealed yesterday.

The thirty-four-year-old, who was a postgraduate from Cambridge University, was sacked by Allegra Knight Skincare Company (AKSC) on October 30. He has not been seen since.

Local police confirmed they wish to speak to him about the theft of a laptop, confidential lab books and equipment from the company.

Former colleagues in Cambridge say his disappearance is out of character. He had been working as a research scientist at the global beauty firm for six months.

Allegra Knight, founder of AKSC, said: "We are extremely worried about Sam Bishop. Our thoughts are with his family and friends."

Miss Knight was the first ever "supermodel" in

the early 1970s and a muse for every major designer,
including Chanel, Givenchy, Valentino and Christian
Dior.

She retired from modelling in the 1980s and
disappeared from public life before launching AKSC
five years ago.

Jessica reread the newspaper article and clicked back
to the photograph, intrigued. *Why was the intruder
interested in you, Sam?*

The young man smiled back enigmatically, refusing
to give up his secrets. She decided to take a copy of
everything to show her dad what had been accessed
and hit "print". As she closed the files, her eyes were
drawn to a tiny thumbnail folder at the bottom of
the screen. She clicked on to it and waited for it to
open. That was odd. The file had no date. It just
existed, which was impossible. It must have come from
somewhere. Encrypted pages suddenly appeared on the
screen – random numbers and letters, apart from the
words *Sam Bishop* and *Starfish*, which stood out.

She plugged her dad's external scanner into the
computer and did a more detailed search on its origins.

She tapped her fingernails on the desk, or what was left of them. They were bitten down and one had started to bleed. She hadn't realized she'd picked it. She jumped as she heard a noise. Was that the lift? She half-expected the intruder to jump out again, but it was just the central heating coming on upstairs.

Calm down, Jessica.

The info flashed up on the device. The file had been uploaded today at 12.32 p.m., the time of the break-in. She stared back at the computer screen, stunned. Had the intruder planted this on her dad's hard drive? Why would they do that?

She tried to click open the toolbar but the mouse wasn't working. She jiggled it about, back and forth, but nothing happened. Suddenly, the cursor moved across the computer screen even though she wasn't touching the mouse any more. It clicked on the top right-hand corner and closed the file. Someone had taken over control of the computer. She tried to move the mouse again but the cursor hit the "shut down" command and the computer logged off. She flopped back in her chair.

Ohmigod.

Someone had got into her dad's computer. They must have been alerted as soon as she logged on and somehow piggybacked their way into the programme without her noticing.

Someone, somewhere, was watching her every move.

CHAPTER FIVE

Jessica jumped as her mobile rang. It flashed up PRIVATE NUMBER.

"Hello?"

"Jessica!"

"Dad! I've been trying to get hold of you. Someone's—"

He cut in, his voice barely a whisper but urgent.

"Code Red."

The line went dead. "Dad?"

She didn't have time to panic. Quickly, she dialled the number he'd made her memorize. She'd never had to use it before. It was a system her dad had devised when ringing 999 wouldn't be enough. She had to dial the number and give the code. She had no idea who or what was at the other end but guessed it must be connected to MI6. It gave eight rings.

"Hello?" a man said sharply. "Hello. Who is this?"

"I'd like to order a dozen white roses," Jessica said mechanically.

"What?" His voice was low and gravelly.

Something about it made Jessica pause. "I said I'd like to order a dozen white roses."

The man took a sharp intake of breath. "You've got the wrong number. This isn't a florist."

"It can't be the wrong number, I dialled it right. Dad gave me this number."

The man paused for a split second. "Your dad gave you the wrong number. Don't call again."

The line went dead.

"No!" She slammed the phone down on the desk. She'd dialled the right number, she knew she had. Why hadn't he helped? Code Red was her dad's signal that he was in mortal danger. Anything could have happened.

She had to find him.

She looked about the room. She couldn't risk

alerting the hacker by using any of her dad's equipment. But she could track him through his credit card; she had an online banking app on her phone. She clicked on a bookmark and brought up her dad's account. She knew his passwords from helping with the accounts and easily called up his last few transactions. He'd bought a Saturday morning Eurostar ticket to Paris and paid for a week upfront at the Hôtel Relais Saint-Jacques. He'd also been in Paris early last week – staying in the same hotel and eating in various restaurants and cafés, according to the charges.

He was looking for Sam Bishop.

His hotel was a start. She could try and track him from there. She'd had a Parisian au pair when she was little and could speak French fluently, so getting about on her own wouldn't be a hassle. First, she'd go to MI6 and report everything that had happened. It was the next best thing to Code Red. The security service could alert Interpol and start looking for him. They'd have to do *something*. As she strode into the lift, she noticed something was wrong with the account. It was £503,031 in credit. As if! She hit "refresh" but the figures remained the same. There'd been a £500,000 transfer on Saturday afternoon from a bank in the British Virgin Islands.

How on earth had he managed to earn that much? Did it have something to do with Sam Bishop?

Back in the ground floor study, she quickly texted Becky, telling her she was ill and wouldn't be back for afternoon lessons. She had a quick scout around her dad's bedroom, which contained lots of framed photos of her and Mum. She couldn't find anything useful. He was always pretty careful with work stuff and didn't leave files or gadgets lying around.

She reset the burglar alarm, grabbed her rucksack and headed outside. She let out a cry as she collided with something warm and solid: a man wearing a long black coat. His grey eyes were expressionless; his lips thin and pinched. He stared down at her unblinking, without even the hint of a smile.

Jessica held her breath, her back pressed against the door. Her dad's Code Red message might actually have worked.

"Jessica Cole?"

She nodded, calculating whether she could knock him off guard and get back into the house if he turned

44

out to be the intruder, returning to finish her off. She was a brown belt at kick-boxing. She didn't have enough room to swing a punch but could easily bring her knee up into his groin before sticking a thumb in his eye. They weren't moves that'd help her earn a black belt, but she'd been taught how to use them in dangerous situations. This certainly felt like one of them.

"We're from the Foreign Office. You need to come with us."

He suddenly took a step backwards, as if he'd read her mind and didn't particularly fancy a knee to his nether regions.

"We?" Jessica said.

He nodded over his shoulder.

Another man climbed out of a black Merc parked outside the house.

"I believe you were trying to order a dozen white roses?" he said coldly. "You need to come right now."

So the telephone number was right!

Taking a deep breath, she followed him down the path and climbed into the back seat of the Merc. It had blacked-out windows. The door shut firmly behind her. She knew without even trying that the door would be locked. She couldn't get out. The man slid into the passenger seat.

"Where are you taking me? Do you know where my dad is? How—?"

A dividing screen slid silently up, cutting her off in mid-sentence.

"I guess not. Thanks for nothing!"

She hung on to the door handle as the driver sped through west London. Soon, the River Thames was in sight. The traffic was light and the Merc made fast progress, jumping a few red lights as it glided up the Embankment.

She watched the bridges whizz past and noticed a few barges on the river. It suddenly hit her. She knew where they were going. There was no question. It had to be MI6 HQ. The Merc suddenly swerved off the road.

Now where were they taking her?

She pulled out her mum's pendant from beneath her blouse and rubbed it between her fingers; it always helped calm her down whenever she was feeling stressed. The car slowed down as it approached a shabby-looking building with torn cream shutters and peeling grey paint. The sign "no vacancies" hung in the window below the name Hotel Celeste. The driver aimed towards a sign for underground parking marked GUESTS ONLY. The car glided smoothly beneath the barrier into the bowels of the building and stopped next to another black Merc. She frowned. Both cars looked out of place. This definitely wasn't the type of hotel that had Merc drivers as clientele. Clapped-out Fiesta drivers, maybe.

The door swung open, catching her unawares. Her "minder" moved a fraction of an inch, allowing her just enough room to squeeze out.

"This way." The man jerked his head towards a door.

She followed slowly. As she stepped through the back door, she smelt fresh flowers instead of the reek of damp and fried breakfasts she'd been expecting. It didn't look anything like a hotel either. She couldn't see a reception area or pamphlets lying about detailing London's attractions. The floor was wood panelled and recently polished. She caught a glimpse of a study and a sitting room as she passed by.

"Where are we?"

The man remained silent as he climbed the stairs. She hesitated. She didn't care what the sign on the building said – this definitely wasn't a hotel. Where were all the staff and guests? She remembered what her dad had told her about MI6 safe houses being dotted around the country. Was the hotel sign a cover for one?

She climbed two flights of stairs after the man, taking in the old-fashioned prints of butterflies lining the walls. He paused, out of breath, and cleared his throat as they reached a landing. A corridor stretched to the left and right.

"Second door on the left." The man jerked his head down the corridor. "They'll be ready for you in a few minutes."

"Who will be ready for me?" she shot back.

"I'm not at liberty to say. You won't have to wait long."

She walked towards the door, clenching her fists. She had to be ready for anything. She took a deep breath and walked in. The room smelt strongly of pine furniture polish. In the centre was a long wooden table with a dozen chairs. The pale cream walls were dotted with uninspiring paintings of sea scenes and country cottages.

"Wait here."

She turned around. Mr Personality-Less stood right behind her, invading her personal space again.

"It's been *so* cool meeting you," she said. "We should hang out together soon."

He scowled as he retreated. She half expected to hear the door lock but there was silence. She checked her mobile. Zero network coverage. Who was she going to call anyway? This was her best shot at helping Dad.

She stepped backwards as the door clicked open.

CHAPTER SIX

A woman walked in first. She wore a black trouser suit and a red Liberty scarf, delicately knotted at her neck. She looked like someone's grandmother with her short, white, curly hair and matronly figure – until she gazed at Jessica. Her blue eyes were glacial. A man with close-cropped grey hair and glasses followed her into the room. He wasn't one of her chaperones. Pushing his glasses up his nose, he fished out a sheaf of papers from a brown file and avoided eye contact. Jessica noticed he wasn't as well-groomed as the woman. He had a coffee stain on his shirt and bitten fingernails, like hers.

"Sit down," he said curtly.

"I'd prefer to stand, thanks. I need you to—"

The woman raised her hand to silence Jessica without looking up. She slid into a chair next to the man and pulled her own file out of a briefcase. She read through the documents, torturously slowly, licking her forefinger as she turned the pages. Why couldn't they both get a move on? She needed them to start looking for Dad straight away. She didn't have time to waste.

The man glanced up, fiercely. This time Jessica sank into a chair.

"My name is Nathan Hall and this is Margaret Becker."

"You're both MI6 agents." She hoped she sounded confident. "And you're probably not using your real names. But that doesn't matter. I just need you to help find my dad."

Nathan stared back, expressionless. This was a classic MI6 interview technique. Never fall for the enemy's tricks by confirming their information, but did he think *she* was the enemy?

"Thank you for joining us," Margaret said pleasantly. "We are from MI6 and we didn't feel the need to use false names with you, Jessica. We're all friends here. I'm sorry if Clifford startled you at your house just now. His social skills sometimes leave a lot to be desired."

Nathan glared at her as if she'd somehow gone off script and given away more information than she was supposed to. Jessica glanced at the pair. So this was how it was going to be. Good cop, bad cop. But why were they using interrogation techniques on her?

"Let's cut to the chase," Nathan said. "Where's your dad?"

"I don't know exactly. He didn't say."

"So you've spoken to him today?"

Jessica had the distinct impression she wasn't telling him anything he didn't already know. Nathan pushed his glasses up his nose again and waited, fingers drumming impatiently on the table.

"He rang about forty-five minutes ago and said Code Red. I dialled a number he gave me."

Nathan flinched slightly.

"So that was *you* on the phone. Why did he want me to call you? Do you know Dad? Have you any idea where he is?"

"We're asking the questions, not you," Nathan said curtly. "Now, let me get this straight. You followed your dad's instructions but didn't think to ask why he needed your help?"

"He was cut off before I could ask him."

"You see, neither of us believe that. We think he gave you more instructions."

"If he had, I swear I'd tell you."

"Not if he'd trained you to keep quiet, and he has trained you well, hasn't he, Jessica?" Nathan leafed through her file. "You're becoming quite the little spy: planting listening devices in a suite in The Ritz and pretending to be ill so you could gain entry to a house in Knightsbridge. What were you up to there, I wonder?"

Jessica reddened. She'd been helping her dad out when he felt too ill to work alone. She'd planted a bugging device to help catch the vice president of a pharmaceutical company who was suspected of industrial espionage. She felt sure MI6 had found this out already.

"Not so keen to tell us now, are you?" Nathan said. "So you can see why we have a few problems trusting someone who's been trained to do exactly as her daddy says. What has he told you to do now? Tough it out with us and wait for him to get in touch with another code word? Then you'll go to him in a few weeks' time, right?"

"If I knew for certain where he was in Paris, I'd go to him right now."

The words slipped out before she could stop them.

"So he did tell you where he is." Nathan banged his fist on the table.

"No. I saw his bank account. He'd paid for a Eurostar ticket and checked in at the Hôtel Relais Saint-Jacques. I'm pretty sure he's looking for a missing scientist called Sam Bishop."

Nathan and Margaret exchanged glances.

Jessica shifted in her seat. Was it her imagination or was the room really hot? The radiators must be on full blast. She'd kill for a glass of water but they weren't offering.

"What's going on? I just want you to start looking for my dad. He's in danger."

A sinister look crept across Nathan's face. "Your dad's a traitor and a murderer."

"No way! That's ridiculous." Her voice sounded weird and a long way away.

"We wish we were mistaken. It would make things a lot easier." He jerked his head at Margaret. "Show her."

Good cop slid a bank statement towards her. "Perhaps you can explain why five hundred thousand pounds was transferred into your father's bank account on Saturday afternoon from the British Virgin Islands?" She pointed to the transaction with a soft-pink-lacquered nail.

Jessica rubbed her forehead. Her dad couldn't possibly have earned that much. He didn't earn a fraction of that amount on jobs.

"No. I can't explain that exactly. Except, I think—"

"But *we* can explain," Nathan interrupted. "Your dad was paid by this man, via an offshore bank account, to locate and deliver Sam Bishop."

He pushed a grainy black and white photo towards her. It showed a dark-haired man who was wearing a pale-coloured suit and sunglasses. She tried not to show any reaction as Nathan studied her. It was the photo she'd seen in one of the MI6 files, lying on the floor in her dad's bunker.

"Vectra is one of MI6's most wanted men – a

terrorist with links across the Middle East, Algeria and Libya," Nathan said. "He has a fanatical interest in adapting scientific developments for use in chemical and biological warfare."

Jessica shoved the photo back across the table. "My dad wouldn't have anything to do with a terrorist. You're crazy to think that he would. He was hired by Sam's mum. I saw the file on Dad's computer."

Margaret raised an eyebrow as she flicked through the file again. "Do you really think a retired schoolteacher could rustle up five hundred thousand pounds *and* have access to an offshore bank account? Isn't it far more likely that your father took on the case for Mrs Bishop and then sold Sam when he realized how much Vectra would pay for him?"

Jessica shook her head vigorously. This was totally insane. Why wouldn't they listen?

"We intercepted a number of coded messages between Vectra and someone called Starfish, discussing Sam," Nathan said brusquely. "We have very compelling evidence that your dad's secret codename is Starfish."

Jessica's eyes widened. Starfish. The name from the file the intruder had uploaded on to Dad's computer.

There was probably more incriminating data planted on there too.

"Do you recognize the name Starfish?" Margaret leant closer, frowning. "Have you heard your father refer to it before?"

Damnit. She had to be more careful. They were trained to interpret her tiniest of reactions. She must stay cool. "Of course not. Dad takes on lots of missing-person cases – Sam's no different."

"Except this is very different," Nathan persisted. "Starfish has been pretty busy, hacking into MI6 files containing the names of current agents, presumably to sell to Vectra. Their lives are now in great danger."

Jessica didn't betray her feelings this time. She stared straight ahead.

"Dad would never, ever betray his country or MI6. He was one of you!"

"I know this is a shock," Margaret said softly. "It's a shock for us too. We didn't want to believe this about your father either. We both used to work with him. He was a good agent – a good man – back then."

Jessica felt tears prick her eyes and blinked them away. She was talking about him in the past tense, as if he were dead. "He still is a good man. A really good man."

"But things can change," Margaret said. "Don't you think your father could have been tempted by the cash? Isn't it possible he's securing your financial future when the multiple sclerosis finally leaves him unable to work?"

"Never!"

Nathan shuffled his papers. "MI6 – or rather I – warned your dad to stay away from this case, but he didn't listen. He returned to Paris on Saturday, at around the same time that Vectra flew in. He made contact with one of our agents who'd been assigned the Sam Bishop brief after we learnt of Vectra's interest."

He pushed a colour photo towards her. Jessica recognized the beautiful redhead instantly.

"But that's Lara Hopkins, the face of Mulberry," she blurted out.

"Your dad arranged to meet her to discuss Sam later that afternoon."

Nathan passed her another grainy picture which had been taken from a CCTV camera at 3.02 p.m. A couple sat at a table, holding coffee cups. She instantly recognized her dad even though she could only see his profile. Lara's hair was scraped into a knot and she was wearing a light-coloured raincoat.

"Lara's a spy?" She couldn't quite believe it. She was the face of half a dozen fashion houses, including Louis Vuitton and Marc Jacobs.

"*Was* a spy," he corrected. "One of our best. Later that night this picture was taken."

He shoved a third photo in front of her. This time Lara lay in a crumpled heap, her red hair strewn across a green carpet.

"Ohmigod. What's happened to her?"

"She was found strangled in her hotel room," Nathan said grimly.

Jessica pressed her fingers to her lips as her stomach churned horribly. This was probably just routine for him, but she'd never seen a dead body before. Somehow, recognizing Lara made it even worse.

"Of course, that's not what we'll tell the press," Nathan continued. "The newspapers will report tomorrow that she was stressed about the start of Couture Week and suffered a fatal asthma attack."

The room lurched. She gripped the table as Nathan

continued. "We think Lara managed to track down Sam and made the mistake of telling your dad his location. Then he killed her before she had chance to report back to us."

Jessica tasted bile rising in her throat. She pushed the photo away. She couldn't bear to look at it. "He didn't do it." Her voice cracked. "Just because he met her doesn't mean he killed her."

"True," Nathan said. "But we've found further incriminating evidence on his computer that links your dad, Starfish, to Vectra."

She looked from one to the other. They weren't even considering the possibility it had been planted to incriminate him.

"You need to stop protecting your father right now and cooperate with us," Margaret said. "When has he arranged to get in touch with you again?"

Her tone was as hard as Nathan's. She'd given up playing good cop.

"You're both wrong! Dad's been set up." Her chair toppled over as she leapt to her feet. "Someone's planted all this evidence and you're too blind to see it. Or you just don't want to see it."

She quickly recounted what had happened that afternoon, including the attack and the MI6 files conveniently left in the bunker, waiting to be discovered, along with the encrypted file on the computer.

Nathan's brow furrowed. "You're sure someone was in the house? Absolutely certain?"

"Do you think I imagined being knocked out with chloroform? Or do you just think I'm a liar like my dad? In fact, don't bother answering that. I'm done here. I'll find out where Dad is myself since you're not going to help."

She stalked to the door, but Nathan had already jumped up and blocked her exit. "You're to leave well alone and that's an order."

She glared at him. "So you can fit him up quietly? Not likely!"

He grabbed her arm. "Your dad might let you play detective, young lady, but that's not going to happen now. Stay out of this. You're in way over your head."

She shook him off, curling her fingers into fists. "Get your hands off me!"

"Calm down, Jessica," Margaret said. "This isn't helping anyone. I promise you we'll re-evaluate all the evidence in light of what you've told us. You've been very helpful. But the best thing you can do is go back to school and inform us if you hear from your father again. We'll contact you if we need to speak."

Jessica brushed past Nathan and threw open the door.

"We'll be watching your every move," he called after her. "Don't even think about going to Paris. We have eyes and ears everywhere."

She slammed the door behind her. Hard.

CHAPTER
SEVEN

Jessica clenched her fists as she sat in the back of the Merc. She was so angry she could scream. How could they think that about Dad? He'd never betray MI6 or his country. He always clammed up whenever she tried to talk to him about his time with the security service. He wouldn't divulge secrets to her. There was no way he'd give it all up to a terrorist. He was the most honourable, patriotic person she'd ever met.

She didn't care what Nathan said. She was going to save Dad and clear his name, without MI6's help. She had to. This was what she'd been trained to do.

As the car sped back along the Embankment, she had an idea. She knocked on the glass partition and waited for it to slide down.

"I need to drop by my agency. I've got an appointment with my booker. Can you take me there, please?'

The driver gave a curt nod as she gave him the address. The car peeled off the road and nipped through side streets towards Covent Garden.

The Merc waited outside Primus' offices as she ran up the white stairs. She passed the large black and white photos of some of the agency's most famous models – Taja, Albany, Domenica and Vita. The reception was buzzing as usual. Bookers talked loudly to clients through their headsets while a few leggy models sat on the blue sofas, flicking through their portfolios and fashion glossies. This was one of the few places she didn't feel like a total freak. She definitely wasn't the tallest girl in the room for a change. She felt quite small compared to the Amazonian models who stalked past.

"Look what the cat dragged in!" a voice shrieked.

Michael pulled off his telephone earpiece and reached over the counter to give her an air kiss on each cheek.

"Darling, I *lurve* your school uniform." He wrinkled his nose sarcastically. "But somehow I don't think you'll need it on a shoot any time soon. And what's that sticking in your hair?"

He raised a plucked eyebrow as he pulled out a shred of paper. "Do you know what a comb is these days?"

"I know, I know, I look awful." She smoothed her hair behind her ears and looked down. Her skirt was dusty from the study floor. "Is Felicity here? I need to see her right now."

"She's in her office, darling. But she's going to have an aneurysm when she sees the state of you. You look like you've been dragged through a hedge backwards."

"Thanks." For nothing. He wouldn't look picture perfect either if he'd been attacked. She strode over to her booker's office and hovered at the door. A silver-haired woman in her fifties flicked through photos at her desk while talking loudly into her earpiece. She looked up, grinning, and gestured for Jessica to come in. She sat on the edge of a red chair, waiting for Felicity to finish.

"Jessica, darling! How are you?" Felicity tore out

her earpiece.

She was tempted to say she'd had the worst day of her life. She'd been assaulted, something terrible had happened to her dad and MI6 thought he was working with a notorious terrorist. It was far simpler just to lie.

"I'm fab, thanks, but we need to talk. Can you get me a casting for Couture Week or anything else going on in Paris this week? It looks buzzing."

Felicity looked startled. "I thought you said your dad was really strict and wouldn't let you take days off school to model?"

Jessica smiled gratefully at Roberta, who popped in and passed them each a hot chocolate. She felt guilty for lying to Felicity but had no choice. She needed to get to Paris ASAP and the Eurostar booking and accommodation would be in the agency's name, not hers.

"He's had a change of heart – besides, he'll be there on business anyway," she said, almost too convincingly. "So can you do it?"

Felicity hesitated and ran a hand through her hair, making her chunky amber bracelet jangle.

"I love your enthusiasm, darling, but I'm not sure

you're ready for couture just yet. I wanted to build up your portfolio before we start doing the shows. They're such a catfight, you know that. The designers pick more experienced girls who can take whatever's thrown at them."

"But I can too," she said. "I'm ready, I know I am. I want a shot at it."

Felicity stared curiously at her. "Is everything all right, darling?"

She wanted to scream "No!" at the top of her voice. "Of course. Everything's cool. Surely the shoot with Sebastian and other magazine spreads have raised my profile? I know I haven't got a *Vogue* or *Tatler* cover—"

"Not yet!" Felicity said. "But you will."

"Thanks. That's why I think we should seize this opportunity right now instead of waiting another year. I could also do with the cash."

Felicity drummed her fingers on the desk. "It's late notice to try and get anything for this week. Most of the go-sees have already taken place."

"Please, Felicity, I'm begging you. When my dad sees this month's mobile bill he'll ground me until I'm old and crumbly. Well, at least until I'm thirty."

Felicity burst out laughing. "OK, my little spring chicken. I can't promise the shows, but you're right, there's lots going on in Paris this week. Sara's already out there and had a callback for a job with AKSC just today."

"Allegra Knight's company?"

"That's right. They're launching a new product this week, apparently. *Très* exciting and *très* hush-hush."

"Can I get a casting too?"

Please, please, please. This would be beyond perfect. Sam's mum had asked Dad to visit AKSC. They might have some info about him if he'd turned up, like how he seemed and where he said he was going next.

"I'd love to meet Allegra Knight," she added. "She sounds really cool. I'm sure I could learn a lot from her."

"She was fabulous in her heyday, darling," Felicity said. "You don't get supermodels like that any more. Let's give this a whirl. I'm thrilled your dad's had a change of heart."

"Thank you! You won't regret it, I promise."

Felicity put her earpiece in and started calling all the couture houses, begging for late slots as Jessica sipped her hot chocolate.

Thankfully, Felicity hadn't asked too many probing questions. Jessica wasn't sure how many more interrogations she could take in one day.

Half an hour later, Felicity ripped out her earpiece and pushed her chair back with a broad smile.

"Mission accomplished, darling! You were right. News of your work with Sebastian has spread and you're in demand."

"With AKSC?"

"I haven't heard back from them yet, sorry. I think they may be set on Sara."

"Oh." Typical. That would have been way too convenient.

"Don't look so depressed. I have landed you some last minute go-sees *and* a shoot for *Étoile* magazine on Wednesday morning. Luckily, a few models cancelled and they really wanted you."

Jessica jumped up and gave her a hug. AKSC would have been beyond brill, but this was a good start. At least it got her to Paris. "You're a star, thank you."

"You should thank Emerald as well," Felicity said, with a loud cackle.

"Why?" She stared at her, puzzled. Emerald was Primus' biggest rival.

"All the designers are in a total spin after Emerald's supermodels dropped out of the shows."

"You mean Lara Hopkins?" Jessica shuddered.

"No. Why would she drop out?" Felicity looked confused. "She's big news."

Of course! The supermodel's death hadn't been made public yet. "Sorry, she was the first Emerald model who came to mind. Who do *you* mean?"

"Oh, you know: Darice, Valeriya and the rest of the famous five. You must have read about them all quitting? It's created a gap at the top, which is great news for young girls like you. You'll be able to come up through the ranks much quicker."

Jessica had completely forgotten about the famous five. "What's going on with them anyway?" she asked.

"I've no idea," Felicity stretched back in her chair. "They seem to have vanished off the face of the earth.

No one's heard a peep from them. Obviously I'd be having a fit right now if they worked for me but it's Emerald so I'm pretty chilled."

"Still, it's pretty odd, don't you think?" Jessica threw her rucksack over her shoulder, preparing to leave. "They all decided to quit at the same time and they've completely gone to ground."

Felicity laughed. "Well, if you met Lydia Hollings, you'd probably understand why. She's a nightmare to work for. Nothing like me, of course. I'm your dream boss – a total pussycat."

Jessica managed a small smile. She didn't dare disagree with this particular pussycat. She had *very* sharp claws.

Felicity checked her watch. "You need to scoot now, Jessica. I've got a conference call with New York starting in five. I'll get Roberta to book you on to Eurostar tomorrow morning and email everything over, along with details of the jobs. She's going to have to sort out a legal waiver to allow you to take part in the shows, as well as a female chaperone."

Jessica rolled her eyes. "Really?" That was all she needed. A chaperone would seriously get in her way. She'd have to find a way to dump her at the first opportunity.

"I know, I know, you're a big girl and this will cramp your style, blah, blah, blah," Felicity said, laughing. "But it's necessary for fourteen-year-olds, even for rat-haired ones like you, so there's no point arguing with me. You'll need to catch up on the schoolwork you miss too."

"I understand."

"I'm glad to hear it. Remember to put some make-up on and leave your *brushed* hair down for the castings. You know how important first impressions are. If you look anything like you do today, you won't even get as far as showing your portfolio or your walk. You'll be out the door."

"I'll make an effort," Jessica said.

"Great, because all our reputations are on the line with this. Don't forget that, please."

"I won't." Jessica blew her a kiss as she left. She'd just made getting to Paris a lot easier. She'd worry about the rest later. She ran down the stairs.

The Merc was still waiting outside, its engine running.

The car dropped Jessica off outside her house. She ran up the path without looking back and let herself in. She rested against the door with her eyes shut.

"Where on earth have you been, Jessica? The school rang me to say you didn't turn up this afternoon!"

Uh-oh. Her eyes flew open. A statuesque women with cheekbones that could cut glass glared at her. She was clad in a pink Chanel suit, her white hair coiled into an elegant chignon. She didn't look like most grandmas and certainly didn't appreciate being called one either. She still had the poise and figure of a model despite being in her seventies.

"Not now, Mattie!"

"Excuse me! I'm waiting for an explanation, young lady. Have you been off visiting a boyfriend I don't know about?"

She wished. "No. I felt ill, that's all, and walked about a bit until I felt better." The lies rolled off her tongue easily now. She'd been getting a lot of practice in today.

"I'd have picked you up if you'd called," Mattie said. "I've been worried sick. Do you have any idea what's been going on here today?" She gestured towards the study, her diamond and sapphire rings glittering.

Jessica shook her head. It wasn't a good idea to admit what she knew if she wanted to get to Paris tomorrow. Mattie would never let her go if she fessed up to everything, particularly the bit about being knocked out with chloroform.

"Spooks have been crawling all over the house!" Mattie's tone was outraged but she still couldn't bring herself to say "MI6". She barely acknowledged her dad's former career. "They've taken goodness knows what from your father's study. Did you know he has a secret underground bunker?"

Jessica looked away. She wasn't in the mood for another confrontation.

Mattie folded her arms in exasperation. "What am I saying? Of course you did! Your father involves you in *everything*."

So they *were* going to revisit this old argument. Mattie had hit the roof when she'd found out Jessica's dad had taken her on a surveillance job last month. She hated her getting involved in spying missions. She thought she was too young, but she was wrong.

"Don't blame Dad. I go down there when he's away and mess about with some of his stuff. He doesn't know."

Mattie sniffed, unconvinced. "Really? So he didn't teach you how to plant bugs and pick locks as soon as you turned thirteen? That was a really helpful birthday present. Most teenage girls get clothes and make-up."

Jessica ignored her dig. "What was MI6 here for, anyway? Did they say?"

Mattie shook her head. "Not a word. They came with search warrants and stripped the bunker downstairs and the study. God only knows what your father's got messed up in this time, but he must be in almighty trouble."

Jessica bit her lip. That was the understatement of the year.

Mattie looked at her curiously. "I've been trying to get hold of him all day. Have you managed to speak to him?"

Jessica hesitated. "Yes. Briefly. He's in Paris on a job. He wants me to join him tomorrow. My agency's lined up some castings and Dad said it'd give us a chance to spend time together."

It was frightening how easily the lies just kept coming. She was pretty much a pro at deceiving people.

"What? Jack doesn't mind you missing school?"

OK, so Mattie wasn't a total pushover.

"I promised I'd do some schoolwork while I'm over there."

"This doesn't sound like Jack. Not at all. I'm going to try calling him again." She reached for her cream Chanel handbag.

"You won't be able to speak to him," Jessica said. "He's gone undercover. He said to tell you that MI6 might turn up but not to worry. It'll blow over."

Mattie put her handbag down again with a contemptuous snort. "Typical. Now that *does* sound like Jack. Sticking his head in the sand and hoping the problem will go away as usual!"

"That's not what he's doing, honest."

"Really? Then why hasn't he come back? Does he just expect me to sort out his mess for him? I have a life too, you know."

Jessica's bottom lip trembled. "Why can't you just leave him alone for once? You're always having a go at him!"

Mattie looked taken aback. "I'm just pointing out that he should be here, getting to the bottom of this problem, rather than encouraging you to miss school,

76

particularly when you're not feeling well. You look really pale and tired." She reached out to touch Jessica, something she never normally did. She wasn't big on showing affection. "I just want to understand what's going on."

Jessica stepped away. "Just leave it, why don't you?" She grabbed her rucksack and climbed the stairs three at a time. She banged her bedroom door shut and slumped on to her duvet, hugging her pillow.

"I'm coming, Dad. I promise."

CHAPTER EIGHT

Jessica had managed to dodge Mattie at breakfast but she was standing guard at the front door, immaculate as usual in a charcoal Chanel suit and pearls, her jewelled fingers glinting under the hall light. Jessica braced herself for another almighty row.

"I'm sorry I upset you yesterday," Mattie said abruptly. "I didn't mean to."

She hadn't been expecting *that*. "I'm sorry too."

"I was trying to say you've had to grow up too quickly through no fault of your own," Mattie continued. "You're used to looking after other people, but you need looking after too."

"I feel fine today, honestly," Jessica said. She pulled on her pea coat and fastened the buttons.

"It's no biggie. It was just a bad day. For both of us."

"That's true." Mattie's eyes misted up as she helped her with a button she'd missed. "You know, you remind me so much of your mother, especially when we quarrel."

Jessica stared at her, surprised. Mattie never usually let her guard down. She and Dad usually found it too difficult to talk about Mum. She'd died in a helicopter crash when Jessica was four. Jessica only got snippets now and then.

"Am I really like Mum? How?"

"Well, you look just like her. She'd never back down in an argument, and I was *always* nagging her to tidy her room."

"What else?"

Mattie fiddled with her sapphire ring. "She was very determined. She talked me into letting her start modelling as a teenager, the way you did with your father. She tried to hide her detentions from me too." She smoothed the wrinkles out of her suit. "But I always found out."

Jessica laughed. "Don't worry about that. It was

just Hatchet Hatcham throwing his weight around as usual. You know how he is when I'm late."

"Well, you don't want to be late today," Mattie said, checking her gold Cartier watch. "At least you've got morning lessons before you have to leave for Paris."

Jessica winced. That was yet another lie she'd told Mattie yesterday. But what could she do? She had to pretend to go to school in case anyone was following her. Hopefully, they'd give up when they thought she was sticking to her normal routine and heading to lessons. Her train was actually leaving at 10.25 a.m. and she wouldn't be at registration.

Mattie handed her an envelope stuffed with hundreds of euros. "I know your hotel bill's already paid for, but this is some extra in case you need it. No arguing, I insist."

"Really? That's so generous. Thank you." Jessica threw her arms around Mattie and closed her eyes. She hadn't hugged her grandma for a long time. She smelt of roses. A memory of her mum came flooding back. Even though her name was Lily, she preferred roses. She used to fill the house with vases of them.

"There, there," Mattie said, pushing her back. "You know I'm still not happy with you travelling alone.

I'd much prefer to meet you at school and take you to Paris myself this afternoon."

"Honestly, it's fine. I travel on the Underground by myself all the time. The Eurostar's no different. Plus I've got a chaperone at the other end and Dad's already in Paris."

That wasn't a lie. It just wasn't the whole truth.

"I suppose so." Mattie didn't sound convinced.

"It's cool. You were travelling around by yourself at my age. This isn't so very different."

Mattie gazed at her. "You have no idea." She handed over her large Louis Vuitton overnight bag – a gift from a recent shoot – and school rucksack. "Remember to be careful and call me at least once a day."

"I will. I promise." She opened the door and walked down the black and white mosaic path.

"Wait, Jessica!"

She turned back.

Tears had formed in Mattie's eyes. "You'd tell me if something was wrong, wouldn't you?"

"Of course." The lie lingered in the air as she walked up the street.

*

Jessica reached the school gates after a detour and crouched down. She fumbled with her rucksack straps, pretending she'd forgotten something. She pulled a mirror out of her pocket and used it to check over her shoulder. She'd tried to shake off the black Merc but it was still on her tail. It pulled over further down the road, its engine running.

She stood up and quickened her pace, marching into the deserted playground. Suddenly, someone pounced and enveloped her in a rough bear hug. Her arms were pinned to her body.

"Got you!" a voice snarled.

Jessica threw her head back. There was a crunch as she made contact with a chin. She kicked back, scraping her heel down a shin, and jabbed her right elbow into the solar plexus. The hands released her and she spun round, feeling the satisfying crunch of bone as her fist slammed into someone's nose.

"Aaaargh!"

Jessica looked down at Tommy Williams, who was writhing at her feet, clutching his nose.

"You!" Jessica exclaimed.

"I think you've broken my nose, you little cow!" he said, spitting out a mouthful of blood.

"You shouldn't have grabbed me like that. I thought you were attacking me. Sorry."

"You will be sorry when I report you and you're expelled." He dabbed his nose.

"It was self-defence," Jessica insisted. "Anyway, do you really want everyone to know you've been beaten up by a girl? It could seriously damage your image of being, you know, a total psychopath."

Tommy hesitated. He shook his head.

"Good." Jessica helped him to his feet. "Let's agree this never happened."

Tommy shook her off and jerked his head.

"I'll take that as a yes." She ran to the bike sheds where Becky was waiting, shivering in a short grey skirt and pullover. The skull-and-crossbones earrings were back in her lobes.

"Did I really just see you deck Tommy Williams?"

"I don't think he'll be jumping out on anyone like that again. I just hope he doesn't report me. He could blow everything."

"Blow what? Why couldn't you ring the doorbell

when you dropped the note off last night? Or just phone me?" Becky touched her arm. "Does this have something to do with why you didn't come back to school yesterday?"

"Sort of." She hadn't been able to risk using her phone or email to arrange a rendezvous with Becky. "I'll tell you everything eventually, I swear, but not yet. It's safer if you don't know at the moment."

"Safer? What do you mean?" Becky's forehead wrinkled with worry.

"There isn't time to explain." She passed Becky the absence note she'd persuaded Mattie to sign. "Please, just hand this into the office."

"Of course I will. I'm worried, that's all—"

"I know," Jessica cut in. "But don't. I'm cool, honestly. Did you bring it?"

Becky fished her iPhone out of her bag and handed it over.

"It's the best birthday present ever," she said. "Try not to lose it. I've got lots of pics on it that I haven't backed up yet."

"I won't, I promise." Now Jessica wouldn't have to use her own phone, which MI6 was undoubtedly

84

bugging. She could monitor it for incoming calls and texts and use Becky's iPhone whenever she needed to make a call. She logged on to Becky's emails: the contact point she'd given Primus. Roberta had already sent a message saying she was booked into Hôtel Keppler by the Champs-Élysées. Camille, her chaperone, would accompany her to the shoot tomorrow.

"Great," she said to Becky. "I need you to do one more thing for me."

"Name it."

"I'm pretty sure a black Merc followed me to school. I need you to distract the driver while I slip out. There's probably a passenger too. They're parked further down the road, on the right."

"Seriously?"

Jessica nodded. "I need you to get rid of them."

"Leave it to me. I'll make it an Oscar-worthy performance. Shame a Hollywood director won't see it."

Jessica smiled. That was what she loved about Becky. She supported her, no matter what, and didn't ask *too* many awkward questions. They walked in silence to the gates.

Becky gave her a quick hug. "Be careful and good luck."

"And you."

Becky strode out. A few seconds later, Jessica heard a scream. She peeped round. Becky was standing by the Merc with her hands on her hips.

"What are you staring at?" she yelled. "Are you a perv or what?"

A couple of builders working on a house nearby looked up.

"Are you all right, love?" one shouted.

"No. These guys are harassing me. They said they'd pay me a tenner if I let them look up my skirt!"

The builders strode over as a man climbed out of the passenger side. It was Clifford. This was her chance. She shot out and veered left down the road. She looked over her shoulder as she turned the corner. A builder pulled the driver out of the car and punched him while his mate wrestled Clifford to the pavement.

Hoorah! Her plan had worked. Now she was out of sight, she broke into a run until she reached the main road. She hopped on a bus. She peered out of the window, but she couldn't see anyone in pursuit. A few stops along she jumped out and switched to the Underground in case she was being followed. From there, it was a straightforward journey to St Pancras International station.

She found the toilets and locked herself into a cubicle. She hurriedly pulled on a pair of faded skinny jeans, a cream Topshop sweater and a black aviator-style leather jacket and boots. She stuffed her uniform into her rucksack and let herself out. She splashed some water on to her face and stared in the mirror. She didn't see a model staring back, or a spy. Just a scared, stupid teenager.

What the hell did she think she was doing? She was used to going on jobs with her dad but this was different. She was alone. This was all down to her. She didn't have any backup.

She dabbed on some lipgloss and applied her eyeliner and mascara. The war paint made her feel braver. She could do this. She *had* to do this. She walked back, gripping her online ticket, and joined the long queue snaking away from the security checks. The atmosphere was tense as a school party held everyone up. Boys and girls squealed with excitement and dodged about, getting underneath everyone's feet as their rucksacks passed through the X-ray scanners.

She tagged after them to passport control. The harassed-looking man on the desk waived the party through and sighed irritably as she walked up. She handed over her passport and smiled. The man gave it a cursory glance.

"Good luck. You're going to need it," he muttered. "Go through."

"Thank you."

She hadn't flagged up any security alerts. He obviously thought she was one of the teachers' helpers. She still had a few minutes spare, so she bought a croissant and a caramel frappuccino before boarding. No one looked up as the carriage door slid back.

Jessica found her seat quickly; the train was quiet so she had a table to herself. A man in a business suit tapped away on his laptop in front. To her left, a thirty-something woman in a smart black trouser suit flicked through a discarded glossy. She paused over a fashion spread, long enough for Jessica to catch a glimpse of a moody-looking girl clad in a

88

bead-embellished gold maxi dress from Marni and a Religion black leather jacket. It was her! That was one of her first major shoots for *Teen Mode*. She'd loved that edgy rock-chick look. It was awesome. The woman looked up and stared. Jessica reddened. Had she recognized her from the magazine or was she an MI6 agent, tailing her?

She pulled out her iPod and stuck in the earphones. This was the only other gadget MI6 had accidentally left behind, apart from her dad's iPad that she'd taken to school. Thankfully, she'd let Mattie borrow it yesterday and no one, not even MI6, dared to look inside her Chanel handbag. She guarded it, Rottweiler-like.

She flicked on the application and pretended to select a track, pointing it in the magazine woman's direction. The mobile and laptop in her brown leather briefcase had normal frequencies and firewalls, as did the businessman's laptop. She swept the whole carriage, just to be on the safe side. Devices belonging to an M16 undercover agent would light up like the Fourth of July due to their complicated security systems. They'd be more protected than Buckingham Palace.

The carriage was clean.

After a few minutes, the train pulled away from the station and she relaxed for the first time all day. Everything had gone to plan so far. Ravenous, she devoured her croissant and washed it down with swigs of frappuccino. She flicked through the agency's emails. Primus had arranged for a car to pick her up from Gare du Nord and forwarded a detailed itinerary, along with her chaperone's mobile. She was free today but the rest of the week looked pretty stacked. She'd have to dodge Camille and probably skip a few castings too. She'd face Felicity's wrath on her return to London.

She flicked open her pendant and stared at the thumb-sized photos of her parents. She took in her dad's kind, tanned face with the strong jaw she'd inherited, the honest blue-grey eyes and short, silver hair. She touched her mum's picture. Mattie was right. She did look like her. They had the same long blonde hair and the gap between their front teeth. This photo had been taken shortly before her death. She didn't remember the crash or the funeral. She only had a few memories: Mum pushing her along on her bicycle;

giving her a raspberry lolly when she grazed her knee; the scent of roses.

She snapped the pendant shut and closed her eyes. She'd lost her mum.

She wasn't about to lose her dad too.

CHAPTER
NINE

"*Pardonnez-moi.*"

Jessica jolted awake.

Someone had accidentally brushed against her, holding a coffee cup. The woman exited the carriage. A passenger sat opposite Jessica, buried behind a copy of the *Financial Times*. She tensed as she looked about. Where had everyone gone? There weren't any stops before Paris but the carriage was empty apart from the person sitting opposite: a man, judging by the hands.

She leapt up. The man lowered his newspaper and folded it neatly in half.

"Which part of the 'you're not allowed to go to Paris' order didn't you understand?" Nathan snapped.

"I thought I'd made myself pretty clear yesterday, or don't teenagers understand plain English any more?"

Ohmigod. She was well and truly busted. She was still debating what to say when he jumped to his feet.

"I'll let you think about that while I buy us both a cup of tea. You look pretty pale. Do you want a sandwich?" He stared icily at her. "I could really do without you fainting on me right now. Or *pretending* to faint."

She shook her head. Judging by the look on his face, he'd probably relish lacing her sandwich with poison.

"Suit yourself." He patted his jacket to find his wallet.

Jessica looked up and down the carriage for an escape route.

"Sit down," he growled. "There's no point trying to run off. We don't arrive in Paris for another hour so there's nowhere to go. I don't want to cause a scene by handcuffing you, but I will if I have to. I've already cleared this carriage to give us some privacy." He gestured to the empty seats before leaving.

She checked her watch. Nathan was right. The toilets were the only place to hide but she couldn't stay locked inside a cubicle for ever. More MI6 agents could be aboard. She couldn't jump from the train either. At this speed, she'd never survive. Her best bet would be to try and shake him off when they arrived. She could outrun him in the station.

After a couple of minutes the door slid open and Nathan reappeared, frowning hard. His black mood clearly hadn't lifted. His mobile was clamped to his ear and a white paper bag swung from his other hand.

"I want results, not excuses," he barked into his phone. "Do your job or I'll find someone who can."

He hung up and tossed the phone on to the table. He passed her a paper cup without looking at her and sat down.

"I expect the tea tastes like mud but it's the best I can do."

She watched as he unpacked his own cup and some sandwiches. He shoved a packet across the table towards her.

"I thought you might have changed your mind," he said shortly.

"I haven't." She tossed the sandwiches back with equal contempt. "I'm not going home. My agency's lined up some jobs for me in Paris. I'm going to be working flat out over the next couple of days."

"Wow! That's really convenient. Did you persuade them to do that when you swung by after our little talk?" He cracked the knuckles of his right hand.

She winced. "That's my business."

"And yet now it's mine. I had to warn your dad off because he refused to stay away from Paris. He was jeopardizing our operation. Now you're being equally obstructive. When will you Coles ever learn to do as you're told?"

Probably never.

She shivered as he popped the knuckles of his other hand. Her nerves were ragged enough already without having to listen to that godawful sound. She could tell by the smirk hovering on Nathan's lips that it was a deliberate torture.

"I just want to find my dad," she said.

"You need to leave that to us. We're already looking for him. Why do you think I'm going to Paris?"

"To carry on fitting him up for a crime he didn't commit? You and Margaret seem to be doing a pretty good job of that already."

Nathan shook his head. "Margaret's already in Paris, looking for your dad and chasing up potential leads."

Jessica's heart leapt. "Has she found out anything yet?"

"That's classified."

"Yet throwing mud at my dad yesterday wasn't? Neither of you has even considered the possibility that my dad's innocent and got set up, have you?"

Nathan hesitated. "It's an avenue we're exploring."

"Oh great. That gives me lots of confidence. Well, while you're slowly exploring that avenue, I'll get on with what I'm doing."

"No, you will not!" he shouted. He thumped his fist down on the table, spilling his tea.

Jessica jumped. Her eyes narrowed. Who the hell did he think he was?

They glared at each other in silence as the door slid open and a man walked past en route to the refreshments carriage. The door closed quietly behind him.

Nathan leant closer threateningly. "You don't seem to understand the position you're in, Jessica. I'm not here to negotiate with you. You either do as you're told or you're on the first train back to London."

Jessica's eyes welled up. She couldn't go home without finding Dad. She just couldn't.

"I understand why you're doing this, Jessica, and it's commendable that you're so loyal to your dad." His tone was a little softer now. He reached out as if to touch her wrist. "But believe me, it's time to back off."

She snatched her hand back. Pretending to be sympathetic didn't suit him at all. "You don't understand anything! Do you really expect me to stand back and do nothing while my dad's out there somewhere, needing help?"

"That's exactly what I want you to do," Nathan hit back. "You might have tagged along with your dad on some of his jobs but this is a whole different ball game. People – people who are a lot more experienced than you – are ending up dead. Is that what you really want?"

Jessica shivered as she remembered the image of Lara, lying strangled on the floor. Was he threatening her or simply warning her off? It was hard to tell.

"These are the rules," Nathan said smoothly. "I'll

let you stay in Paris as long as you behave yourself. Get on with your modelling and stay out of my way. I've retrieved a copy of your itinerary from Primus's computer system so I'll know where you are every minute of every day. I've also placed an undercover agent close to you. If you don't turn up for something, if you're even five minutes late, they'll report back to me."

"I wouldn't—"

"That's good, because I don't give second chances. You mess up, you'll be going home in handcuffs to meet my boss, Mrs T. I wouldn't recommend that encounter. She's nowhere near as nice as me."

Jessica snorted. *Nice* wasn't a word she'd ever use to describe him. She could think of plenty of other adjectives, though.

Nathan's eyes narrowed as if he could read her thoughts. He gestured to his mobile on the table.

"Does your grandmother even know what happened to you yesterday? Or that your dad's gone completely off the grid in Paris? I can ring her right now and enlighten her. It's your choice. How do you want to play this?"

Choice? She scowled at him. He'd played his trump card. Mattie would kill her if she found out what she was up to. She dreaded her more than the mysterious Mrs T, or even him.

"I can behave myself," she said finally. God, she hated him.

"Good. In return, I'll let you know if I find out anything about your dad." He picked up his paper again.

Jessica stared out of the window. In the reflection, she could see him staring at her with a look of sheer contempt. She didn't believe him for a second. Why would he tell her anything?

CHAPTER
TEN

Nathan shared the car from the station and dropped her off at her hotel. He'd given her a card with his mobile number. Scribbled on the back were the details for his hotel. The Ritz. Clearly expenses weren't an issue at MI6. *Lucky him*. Her hotel wasn't as grand but it was still pretty cool. Her room had funky black and white furniture and a large flat-screen TV. Normally, she'd raid the minibar for chocolate and crisps, watch rubbish soaps for hours and soak in a hot bath, but she couldn't have fun today. She had too much to do.

First, she texted Mattie to say she was OK. It was tempting to text her PFB – Potential Future Boyfriend – too; it hadn't been hard to get Jamie's number after he'd left his mobile lying about in art class. But what would she say to him?

Hiya. I'm in Paris, dodging MI6 and trying to find my dad, who's a suspected murderer/traitor. How r u?

What would she ever say to him?

Stay away. I'm trouble.

She didn't have time for boys – even the best-looking one in the entire universe. She double-checked her dad's mobile. Nothing, still voicemail. She fired up his iPad and did a geolocation trace on the phone. The SIM card had been removed or destroyed so she couldn't pinpoint where he was. However, she could see the locations he'd made calls from over the last few days. He'd used his mobile a lot in his hotel and at a café, where he'd rung both their home phone and Mattie's mobile on Saturday afternoon. It was probably worth a visit to see if the waiters remembered him. She didn't recognize the other numbers – one was a mobile he'd called five times throughout Saturday. He'd made a call to it from AKSC that morning and been on the line for three minutes.

So he *had* paid a visit to the company in his search for Sam.

His last call was to the mystery mobile again, at 11.34 p.m. on Saturday. It was made from a location near his hotel. Could he have been heading back there when something happened? He went missing about the same time as Lara was found strangled in her hotel room, according to the time stamp on the photo of the crime scene. That couldn't be a coincidence.

She pulled out Becky's iPhone, masked her number and rang the mobile. It clicked straight on to voicemail, like Dad's.

"Hi. I can't take your call right now. Please leave a message. Hugs and kisses, Lara."

Jessica quickly hung up. That was spooky, hearing the voice of a dead person, speaking from beyond the grave. It was another piece of evidence that pointed to her dad's innocence, which MI6 had ignored or hadn't bothered to examine. If he'd killed Lara, why would he ring her even after her death? Margaret and Nathan would probably argue that he was giving himself an alibi. But what if he'd been trying to warn Lara before someone got to him too?

She shivered. He'd managed to get away from whoever it was long enough to reach a phone and make a Code Red call. That was slightly reassuring. He was still alive two days after his disappearance. If only she had the number he'd used, she could trace it. But it had flashed up on her phone as PRIVATE NUMBER and she didn't have the technology to try and decipher where he was calling from.

She tossed her hair over her shoulders. She had to stay positive and focus on what she did have – evidence that Lara and her dad had been in regular contact and met their fates at about the same time on Saturday night. She also had important leads to follow up – the café where her dad made calls from and most importantly, AKSC.

She flicked through the documents she'd printed off her dad's computer. Her eyes rested on Sam Bishop's photo. She had to think like her dad and figure out what steps he'd taken to find him. Paying AKSC a visit must be her top priority. She really needed that casting call. She'd have to harass Felicity until she came up with the goods.

First she'd retrace her dad's steps, starting with his stay in Paris: the Hôtel Relais Saint-Jacques. It was a risk. If the undercover agent tailed her and reported back to Nathan, she'd be packed off to London by the end of the day. But this could be the only chance to do some serious snooping before she started modelling. She had to give it a shot. She stuffed Sam's picture into her bag, picked up her leather jacket and slipped out. Nobody gave her a second glance as she strode across the lobby and hailed a taxi outside. So far, so good. No one appeared to be shadowing her.

Just to be extra careful, she paid the driver to go via some sightseeing routes in case she was shadowed. She leant out of the window to take a picture of the Arc de Triomphe, like any other tourist. If anyone *did* happen to be following, they wouldn't sense anything out of the ordinary. She peered at a giant white advertising billboard as the taxi overtook a lorry. TEENOSITY was printed in large black letters, with AKSC and the date *25th Janvier* below.

Interesting. Allegra Knight's new product launch was taking place this Saturday. The billboard didn't feature any models or actresses or give any clues about what it was actually advertising. Felicity had said AKSC's new product was hush-hush. She wasn't exaggerating.

Eventually, the taxi pulled up outside Hôtel Relais Saint-Jacques, a white building on rue de l'Abbé de l'Épée, near the heart of the Latin Quarter. Flower boxes were dotted along the window sills and the doors were flung open invitingly. She paid the driver and looked up and down the street. She couldn't see anyone watching her. She pushed her shoulders back, raised her chin and walked inside. Confidence was the key to success, she'd learnt from previous jobs. If she faltered and looked like she didn't belong in the hotel, she'd be pounced on by security and thrown out within seconds.

The young brunette woman with bright scarlet lips behind the desk was her best bet. The name badge said Anouk Girard. She looked like she'd be sympathetic to a teenager in trouble, whereas the man on her right would probably eat her for breakfast.

"*Bonjour*, Mademoiselle Girard," she said, smiling.

She explained rapidly in French that she was looking for her father, Jack Cole, who'd gone missing. She showed the woman her passport and noticed her flinch.

"I'm so sorry, Mademoiselle Cole," she said. "How can I help you?"

"I need to see Dad's room. He checked in on Saturday morning."

Mademoiselle Girard paused. The receptionist on her right picked up the phone. She shot a look at another man who was locked in conversation with an elderly guest nearby. His name badge stated he was the general manager. She reddened as she stared back at her computer screen.

"Please," Jessica said. "I'm begging you. This means a lot to me."

Mademoiselle Girard nodded. "I understand."

She waited until the manager had shaken the guest's hand and wandered away. "*Suivez-moi.*"

Mademoiselle Girard led her through the foyer, past the luxurious bar and lounges and up the stairs to the first floor. She stopped as they passed through a second set of doors.

"This is it," she said. "Monsieur Cole's room. It's as he left it. The police ordered us not to move anything."

She swiped the door open and stepped back as Jessica walked inside. Room 158 was decorated with ornate, patterned scarlet wallpaper, which matched the spread on the king-sized bed.

"I'll give you some privacy," Mademoiselle Girard said, "but I can't be away from the desk for too long." She closed the door behind her.

Jessica felt a lump rise in her throat as she spotted her dad's silver Omega watch on the desk. It'd been a gift from her mum on his birthday. It was one of his most treasured possessions. He always wore it. She didn't dare pick it up in case the police dusted it for fingerprints. She didn't want to be traced back to this room. She felt a stabbing pain in her chest as she remembered the engraving on the back.

Love you for ever, Lily.

She didn't have much time before Mademoiselle Girard returned. She had to find something that MI6 hadn't thought to look for. Her dad's laptop and mobile were gone but his passport and wallet were on the desk, along with his pills. She slipped the bottle into her bag. He'd need his meds urgently when she found him. No one would miss *them*. She turned around, noticing a photo in a small silver frame on the bedside table. She'd given it to him as a birthday present and he always took it with him on business trips. It was taken a year ago while they were holidaying in Cornwall.

She was grinning, her arms wrapped around his neck. Her dad was laughing too. They both looked so happy. She wished she could remember what they'd found so funny. Somehow, it felt important now.

Mademoiselle Girard tapped on the door and stepped inside. She paused as she looked at the picture.

"It's a lovely photo."

"Thank you. I was just remembering when it was taken. Can I stay a few minutes longer? Please?"

Mademoiselle Girard's eyes flickered around the room. "I have to get back before I'm missed. Close the door behind you when you're finished."

Jessica nodded. She waited for the door to shut and sat on the bed. It'd been fruitless. There was nothing here, except memories of her dad. Somehow, she felt closer to him, surrounded by all his things. Just days ago he'd touched the razor in the bathroom and polished the shoes in the wardrobe. He'd worn his watch.

Where was he now?

She jumped up. She was wasting time. The café was next on her hit list. She took one last look around the room and stepped into the corridor. A maid wheeling a trolley laden with towels and soaps glanced up, startled. Jessica explained in French that she was leaving and strode away.

"Jessica Cole?"

She turned back and stared at the name badge pinned to the maid's blue uniform. She'd never met Marie Dumont before.

"*Oui*. Do you know me?"

"You're the blonde from the photograph in there." The maid nodded at the room. "Your father told me you're a model. He's so proud."

"Thank you." She'd used his name in the present tense, not like Margaret. She squeezed her fingers into the palms of her hands. She hadn't cried yet and wasn't about to in front of a stranger.

"He was a kind man and tipped generously for information," Mademoiselle Dumont said.

"What kind of information?"

"About Monsieur Bishop. He was particularly interested in *him*."

Jessica caught her breath. She'd been expecting her to say she'd told her dad about a good local restaurant or something trivial like that.

"Sam Bishop? You talked to my dad about him?"

"*Oui*, mademoiselle. I told Monsieur Cole everything I know."

Jessica couldn't believe her stroke of luck. "What did you tell him?"

Mademoiselle Dumont remained mute until she fished out twenty euros from her purse. The maid grabbed the note and shoved it into her pocket as two elderly guests brushed past.

"This way." She pushed the trolley along the corridors until they reached Room 126. She swiped her card and pushed open the door.

"The room's been cleaned since Monsieur Bishop left, of course," she said, "but no guest has been in here since. Management's planning a refit of some of the rooms on this floor, including this one."

Of course! Why hadn't she thought of this before? Her dad had deliberately checked into the same hotel as Sam Bishop so it would make it easier to speak to employees without alerting suspicion. He always said cleaning staff were a valuable source of information, as they had a good idea of the guests' habits. Sometimes they even peeked into their belongings.

She walked around the room, looking inside drawers

and wardrobes. Mademoiselle Dumont was right: the room had been thoroughly cleaned and smelt of lemon air freshener. Sam didn't appear to have left anything behind.

"So what did you tell my dad?"

"As I said, your father was a generous man." Mademoiselle Dumont smiled patiently and waited, her eyes resting on Jessica's handbag.

She pulled her purse out again and handed over fifty euros. Mademoiselle Dumont grinned as she pocketed the money.

"Monsieur Bishop left the room in a state as usual the morning he disappeared – clothes scattered everywhere, wet towels on the floor, his shaving kit in the sink. The man lived like a *cochon*, what you English call a pig, *non*? He'd been with us for six months and I don't think he ever picked up a sock. *Il était impossible*."

"That's it?" Jessica slumped on to the bed. She might as well have thrown Mattie's fifty euros out of the window. She'd hoped to find out something more interesting about Sam other than his poor personal habits.

"That's why it was such a surprise to see Monsieur Bishop back in the room later that day," she continued. "I'd never met him before. You see, he was always gone by eight a.m. and returned after I'd finished my shift."

"When did you see him?"

"About three p.m. on October thirtieth."

Jessica raised an eyebrow. How could she possibly be so precise?

"I'm not making it up!" Mademoiselle Dumont folded her arms crossly. "It was the day before my son's birthday and I had to pick up his cake after I finished my shift. That's how I remember it."

"OK, I believe you. So what happened?"

"I was doing my afternoon rounds. Just as I got to his door, Mr Bishop came out with his bags. He gave me such a surprise."

"Did you notice anything strange about him?"

"Not really. He looked shocked to see me too and excused himself. He got into the lift. I went into his room and found he'd packed everything up. That struck me as odd. He was our only long-term guest and housekeeping hadn't told me he was checking out. After that, I never saw him again."

"Did my dad ask you anything else?" Jessica said, peeling off a few more notes.

"He wanted to know if I ever saw any syringes or drugs lying around the room. I said absolutely not. I'd remember something as bad as that."

This was an interesting snippet of information. AKSC had accused him of failing a drugs test. He'd either been careful not to leave traces of his addiction or the allegation wasn't true. Could the French police have been covering something up, as Sam's mum had claimed in her letter?

"I must get on with my rounds now," Mademoiselle Dumont said. "I'm running late."

"Of course."

Jessica was standing up to leave when something beneath the wardrobe caught her eye. She knelt down and fished out a tiny scrap of paper. There were more pieces pushed further back but she couldn't reach them.

"It's rubbish the vacuum missed," Mademoiselle Dumont said. "Here, let me throw it away."

"I don't think it is rubbish."

Jessica looked closer. The paper had been intricately

pleated and folded. She carefully tweaked it and a figure took shape.

"It's a swan!" she exclaimed.

"Monsieur Bishop always made things like that," Mademoiselle Dumont said. "He used to leave them scattered across the floor, along with everything else. Like I said, the man was a *cochon*. Some of the girls got fed up with picking up the bits every day, so they probably just brushed them under there."

"I'll keep it, if you don't mind."

"As you wish." She led her out of the room and closed the door.

"One more thing." Jessica fished into her bag and pulled out the copy of Sam Bishop's photograph. "Is this the man you saw that day?"

She stared at the picture and shook her head.

"No. I already told your father, Monsieur Bishop was much older than this. He was a large man with dark hair. I also told that model all about him too. What was she called now? Laura? No, Lara. She said she was a cousin of Sam's and was trying to find him while she was here for Couture Week. *Très, très* beautiful but a terrible tipper."

Jessica stared after Mademoiselle Dumont as she wheeled the trolley down the corridor. Ohmigod. Lara Hopkins had been here too. Was that why she'd been strangled and Jessica's dad was missing? They'd both discovered someone else had emptied Sam's room. It certainly weakened the French police's theory that Sam had gone on the run. If he had, he'd left with the clothes he was standing in and nothing else. But it didn't explain who was in his room that day, removing all his belongings. What did the man with fair hair have to do with Sam and why did he have all his stuff?

She ran back along the corridor and down the stairs. The foyer didn't have any CCTV cameras but the mystery man wouldn't have left through the front entrance anyway. He'd probably found another way to slip out, unnoticed, maybe through the kitchens. That was where she'd go if she wanted a quick, discreet getaway. As she walked past the front desk, she noticed Mademoiselle Girard finishing a phone call. She was alone. Jessica had to make one final stab at getting info.

"Thanks for all your help today," Jessica said

breathlessly. "I don't suppose you could do one more thing for me, could you?"

"That depends," Mademoiselle Girard said. "What is it?"

"Can you call up some information on another guest for me?"

Mademoiselle Girard frowned and stared at her computer screen. "I'm sorry, I can't. I'd get into a lot of trouble if my manager found out."

"I promise I won't tell anyone. I need to find out about a man called Sam Bishop. My dad was trying to find him. Can you see when he last used his key card? It won't take a minute. Please."

Mademoiselle Girard hesitated and shot a furtive look over her shoulder. "You mustn't tell a soul what I'm doing."

Her long, scarlet nails tapped on the keyboard.

"I've already told the *gendarmes* this information," she muttered. "He left his room at seven thirty a.m. on October thirtieth. He re-entered the room at two forty p.m. and departed again at three p.m. That was it."

"Did he check out?"

Mademoiselle Girard shook her head. "The police

arrived to question him the next day, but he hadn't returned. His account was closed later that week."

"Who closed it?"

"AKSC," she replied. "The company had already paid upfront for the room and simply terminated the account. Now you must leave. My manager's coming back from his break." She nodded at the tall, dark-suited man walking towards them.

Quickly, Jessica pulled out the picture. "Is this Sam Bishop?"

"*Oui*, that's him. Now please go before you get me into trouble."

Jessica flashed a grateful smile and left. It had been worth taking the risk; it wasn't cheap but it'd paid off. Outside, she hailed a taxi and jumped in. As it pulled away, she spotted Nathan and Margaret walking briskly into the hotel. She sank down into her seat. That was close. They hadn't seen her.

She was one step ahead of them yet again.

CHAPTER ELEVEN

Jessica laid out the green silk vintage tea dress she'd found in an antiques shop next to the metallic Stella McCartney number a stylist had loaned her. Which one would give her the confidence to get through tonight? Margaret had rung her room shortly after she'd arrived back after taking a detour past the café her dad had visited. That had drawn a blank. If only she'd hung around longer with the waiters, she'd have missed Margaret's call, ordering her to attend an early dinner at a nearby restaurant. Had she and Nathan found out about Jessica's trip? Mademoiselle Girard or Mademoiselle Dumont could have spilled the beans. She'd be in big trouble if they had. But wouldn't they just pack her off to London straight away? Then again, it could always be a ploy to try and catch her out. They were good at mind games.

Next time – if there was a next time – she'd have to think of an excuse quicker. She plumped for Stella. Her designs had helped spur the British Olympic team on to win fistfuls of gold medals in London. Hopefully the designer's shimmering shift dress would be a lucky talisman tonight and help her fly below MI6's radar at dinner. She slipped on the crystal-studded silver Alexander McQueen pumps another Primus model had discarded in the agency. *Her* feet were too big for them, but they fitted Jessica perfectly.

She curled her eyelashes and then applied black liquid eyeliner and mascara. A dab of cherry lipgloss and she was done. She examined her reflection in the mirror. Perfect. Her armoury was just right. She'd look like a fashion-conscious teenager who was more interested in designer labels and a night out in Paris rather than one who was intent on defying MI6.

She grabbed her vintage black velvet evening bag and black sequin shrug and took one final look in the mirror. Something was missing. She slipped on her mum's necklace, which she'd removed before she took a shower, and the blue crystal flower ring her dad had bought her for Christmas.

"You can do this," she told her reflection. "Becky would tell you to put on an Oscar-worthy performance. You just have to get through tonight and you're home free."

She closed the door behind her, checking it had locked properly. She declined the concierge's offer of hailing a taxi and instead followed directions to the Champs-Élysées. Walking helped calm her nerves until she approached the restaurant, which was tucked in between a couple of bars with outside seating. Her heart beat rapidly as she pushed open the door.

Blast.

She'd mistimed it. She'd dawdled but still arrived first. Maybe they were deliberately late, just to unsettle her. She wouldn't put it past them. A waiter checked the reservation and showed her to their table at the back of the darkened room. He handed her a large menu and disappeared. She read the menu, nibbling her nails, which she'd painted in Chanel's Blue Rebel. They'd never get the message.

She didn't know how she'd get through the evening

pretending nothing was wrong when she'd discovered such potentially explosive information about Sam. Who was the mystery man in his room that day? Could it have been Vectra, the terrorist Nathan had talked about, or one of his henchmen? Were Lara and Jessica's dad targeted because they'd found out about him? How would she manage to keep a poker face for the next few hours?

She couldn't. She rose to her feet, almost knocking over her water glass. She tried to catch her waiter's eye. She'd get him to explain to Margaret and Nathan that she felt ill and had to leave early.

"Jessica!" Margaret weaved in between the tightly packed tables, dressed in a black velvet trouser suit. She smiled warmly, making dimples appear on her cheeks. Jessica had never noticed them before.

"I'm so glad you turned up. I thought you might have had second thoughts and thrown a sickie."

"No, of course not." Her cheeks reddened.

"I'm afraid you'll have to excuse Nathan. He has an urgent matter to attend to."

"About Dad?"

"No. Something on the domestic front."

She sat opposite and picked up a menu. If she'd found out about Jessica's visit to the hotel, she wasn't letting on.

"I'm starving," Margaret said. "Shall we order?"

"Yes, please." Jessica dived behind her menu, glad to avoid any probing questions. Just because Margaret hadn't mentioned her visit didn't mean she hadn't discovered her secret.

"Nice nail polish, by the way," Margaret said. "I love Chanel."

Jessica sank down lower behind the menu. *No way* could she know the make. She was practically a hundred.

After a few minutes, Margaret opted for a rare fillet steak and frites with a half bottle of Pinot noir while Jessica ordered a plate of asparagus ravioli with a side salad and sparkling mineral water. As soon as the waiter disappeared, Margaret whipped out photos of her grandchildren. Ben was two and Matilda, four. Her eyes sparkled as she talked about them.

"They keep me young," she said, chuckling. "Although you must think someone my age is positively ancient."

"Not at all," Jessica said.

"You're a good liar!" Margaret threw her head back and hooted with laughter. "I can see why you're so useful to your father. So why don't you fill me in on what you've been doing today?"

Jessica smiled back. "Sightseeing."

Margaret was far friendlier than yesterday, but Jessica had to keep her guard up. However, Margaret could prove useful to *her*. She topped up her empty wine glass as their waiter returned, carrying two large white plates.

"So have you found anything out about my dad yet?" Jessica asked.

"I'm afraid not," Margaret said, slicing through the steak with a razor-sharp knife. Blood pooled on her plate. "The trail's gone cold for him and Sam. Sorry."

Jessica bit her lip as she prodded her ravioli with her fork. Her appetite had deserted her.

"But you'll be glad to hear that I've managed to persuade my boss, Mrs T, to look at this from a whole new angle," Margaret said. "I have a totally different theory to Nathan's."

Jessica looked up. "How do you mean?"

Margaret placed her knife and fork down. "I've known your father for a very long time. I don't believe he's a murderer or a traitor. I agree with you. I think he's been set up, possibly by someone he's crossed in the past. He'd have made plenty of enemies during his time with MI6. We all have."

Jessica took a sharp intake of breath.

"It's OK," Margaret said, placing a hand on hers. "I'm on your side."

Tears welled in Jessica's eyes. "Thank you. I just needed to hear someone say that. What made you change your mind? You and Nathan seemed so certain yesterday."

"The evidence against your father is a little too convenient for my liking, including the encrypted computer file you found." Margaret examined the label on the back of the wine bottle before pouring herself another glass. "I'm still working on Nathan, but he'll come round to my way of thinking."

Jessica started to tuck into her buttery ravioli, which melted in her mouth. "Do you have *any* new leads?"

"Possibly." Margaret chewed a piece of steak slowly.

"I can help," Jessica insisted. "I speak French and Dad's taught me a lot of useful stuff."

"I know," Margaret said, arching an eyebrow. "I read your file."

"So you know I can handle myself."

"I do, but there are too many risks, and realistically, I'm not sure what a teenager can achieve when *we're* hitting a brick wall." She glanced over her shoulder. "I shouldn't really be telling you this, but we're not sure if Vectra's got Sam already or if either of them are still in Paris."

"Why does he want Sam, anyway? He works for a beauty company."

Margaret dabbed at her mouth with a napkin. After the waiter cleared away their plates, she ordered a crème caramel and Jessica a pot au chocolat.

"Truthfully, we don't know what Vectra's after, and that's what worries us," she continued. "Somehow we don't think a terrorist wants to find a cure for the bags under his eyes or his crow's feet."

"Perhaps Sam's created an explosive mascara or a face mask that detonates in thirty seconds," Jessica suggested.

"I doubt it's as James Bond as that. Sam was highly regarded at Cambridge and published research that could have piqued someone's interest. We're looking into that possibility."

"Do you know what he was working on at AKSC?"

Margaret's eyes gleamed as her dessert arrived. She dipped her spoon in straight away. "That's where we've drawn a blank. Allegra Knight isn't exactly forthcoming with us. Again, it's highly confidential – we're trying to get an agent planted in there, but it's taking time."

"That's where I could help," Jessica said eagerly. "AKSC held castings this week. A model from my agency's been called back for a job. If I get a casting I could have a look around for you."

"That's an idea," Margaret said slowly. "But you're not trained up like our agents."

"I'm still pretty good."

"How good, exactly? I've told you what we know. What have *you* found out?"

Jessica fiddled with her spoon. Could she trust her?

"Don't pretend you haven't been doing any snooping. I wouldn't believe it for a minute. You're Jack Cole's daughter, after all."

She took a calculated risk and outlined what she'd discovered at the hotel. "So you see, AKSC closed Sam's account after someone else cleared his room. He didn't return that day."

"I'm impressed," Margaret said, sipping an espresso. "I'll make sure Nathan re-interviews Mademoiselle Dumont and takes a full statement."

Phew. It wasn't a trick. She didn't seem about to frogmarch her to the station. Nathan wouldn't have reacted so calmly. That was a dead cert.

"Can your agency get you a casting at AKSC this week, do you think?" Margaret said.

"They've tried already but I haven't heard back."

"I may be able to pull some strings."

"You could do that?" Jessica asked.

"You'd be surprised," Margaret said, laughing. "MI6 has fingers in a lot of pies. It'd be a question of getting your portfolio on the right person's desk. It wouldn't guarantee you the job, though. The rest would be up to you."

"I understand. Let's hope they're looking for a blonde."

Margaret paused. "There's also Nathan to think about, of course. He doesn't want you anywhere near AKSC."

"He doesn't have a problem with me staying in Paris as long as I'm just modelling. He wouldn't be able to stop me if I get a job there."

"That's true," Margaret said. "Leave AKSC with me and I'll see what I can do. I'll handle Nathan too. At the end of the day we're all on the same team. He'll realize that, eventually."

"Thanks, Margaret. I really appreciate it."

"You don't have to thank me. I'm just doing my job. In the meantime I need to track down Starfish before MI6 has any further leaks." She beckoned to the waiter for the bill. "If your dad isn't Starfish, we urgently need to find out who is."

Jessica got straight on to her dad's iPad when she returned to her room. She did a quick search on Sam Bishop and Cambridge University. It brought up lots of hits. Sam had published papers and given lectures around the world before he left Cambridge. She clicked on the list of his research. It all involved nanotechnology, whatever that was. She did another quick search on the word to find out its meaning.

"The making of tiny particles, about one-millionth the size of a pinhead," she read aloud.

She flicked back to Sam's research. He was interested in nanotechnology and medical science issues. She pulled up the outline of a lecture he'd given in the United States five years ago, entitled "Nanorobots: A Cure for Cancer?"

It sounds like science fiction, but we believe tiny nanotechnology robots that are invisible to the human eye could be programmed to attack cancer cells, he'd written. *These robots would be inhaled through the nose and travel to the site of a tumour in the colon, stomach, lungs or bowel, simply by attaching themselves to the red blood cells. Nanorobots could be programmed to fight all diseases known to man – AIDS, tuberculosis, cholera. They could even be used for heart attack victims. A nanorobot could monitor the heart, replacing the need for invasive surgery and pacemakers.*

*

It sounded like worthy stuff, so how on earth had Sam ended up working for a beauty company? It was hardly the same as finding a cure for cancer. Why had he sold out? She clicked on an interview he'd given to Cambridge University's student newspaper a couple of years ago. She scanned down. He was hitting out at the funding crisis in British universities.

Successive governments have slashed research budgets, endangering countless scientific projects around the country, he claimed. *Ministers should realize it is impossible to conduct pioneering research without sufficient funds. If the situation continues, it will force scientists like myself into the private sector. Only then will we raise enough funds to pursue our research.*

So Sam was working at AKSC for the cash, and according to his mum's letter, he was planning to go back to Cambridge soon. He must have earned enough to pursue his private nanotechnology research, but what was it, and why had it caught the eye of a terrorist? It must be pretty groundbreaking.

She turned the iPad off. It'd been a good day's sleuthing. She knew her dad's disappearance and

Lara's death were somehow linked to Sam Bishop, who hadn't left Paris voluntarily. If she could track down Sam, she'd probably find clues to her dad's whereabouts too. Hopefully Margaret would be true to her word and get her a casting at AKSC. It definitely looked worth a snoop around.

She texted Mattie to say goodnight, changed into her pyjamas and climbed into bed. Her phone beeped. She smiled as she read the message.

Detention was lonely ;) Where are u?

Becky must have given Jamie her number. She started to text her PFB back but stopped herself. What was she thinking? It was far too risky getting Jamie involved in any of this. She turned off the light and hugged her pillow. She couldn't be distracted. She had Dad to think about. She was getting closer to finding him, she knew it.

CHAPTER
TWELVE

Blood streamed down her neck as the life slowly ebbed out of her body. The vampire was moving in for another bite when a sudden movement in the corner of the room scared him off.

"You're supposed to be biting her, not asking for directions to the supermarket!" a voice yelled in French. "I need you to look dangerous."

The photographer stamped his foot impatiently, making the bloodsucker jump. He bared his teeth more ferociously and lunged at her again. Jessica gagged. Ben's breath smelt revolting. Weren't vampires supposed to be afraid of garlic? He must have eaten a stack of garlic bread last night. She knew he'd been hailed as the new Adonis of the male modelling world with his dark, chiselled good looks, but she was thankful she just had to pretend to be bitten by him. It would have been a lot worse if they'd had to do a fake kiss. Gross!

She moved her neck, which was at an awkward angle. She'd been squeezed into a whalebone corset, voluminous petticoats and a huge, crimson Armani Privé gown that was sprinkled with hundreds of Swarovski crystals. Her face had been powdered chalk white and her lips were a slash of glossy scarlet. More Swarovski diamonds were sprinkled in her hair, which had been curled into ringlets and piled into a towering stack. This was one of the best bits of modelling – wearing clothes she could never afford to buy herself in a zillion years and becoming someone else: a character from a different world.

She sat at a table piled high with cream pastries, pastel-coloured macaroons, cheeses and fruit. Her stomach rumbled. This was torture. She was starving. Out of the corner of her eye, she could see the other models, Sara and Margurita, slumped over the table. They too were being attacked by bloodthirsty vampires during the feast. Thankfully, the photographer worked a lot faster than Sebastian Rossini. She figured they'd all spent longer in make-up and being sewn into their extravagant costumes than actually being on set because he called a wrap thirty minutes later.

"Sorry about that," Ben said, wiping the fake blood from his mouth. "I had a heavy night last night and couldn't concentrate properly. I don't usually need so many directions."

He helped her out of her chair, as she could barely move. Grinning, he exposed a row of perfect, white teeth. He pushed his long black hair behind his ears. His eyes were the darkest blue she'd ever seen. He was Prince Charming-style handsome and he knew it, but Jamie beat him hands down.

No contest.

She shrugged. "It's not a problem."

"I'm heading out on the town again tonight if you're interested," he said. "A whole gang of us are going out. The clubs are great around here. Much better than London."

Yikes. Was he hitting on her?

"Er, I can't, I'm sorry," she said, "but thanks anyway."

"Of course, I forgot. You're off the menu." He winked as he walked off. "For now."

Eeugh. He was good-looking but a creep. Sara, the other model from Primus, didn't seem to mind. He was chatting *her* up now. Sara obviously didn't find his massive ego a deal-breaker. Jessica turned around and spotted Camille in the corner, talking to the photographer and a stylist. How could she get rid of the limpet before the whole day was wasted? Camille had picked up her and Sara from the hotel at five thirty a.m. and taken them both to a series of non-stop castings. Jessica was walking for Saint Laurent, Alexander McQueen and Chanel tomorrow, which was great for her agency but bad news for her. It meant she couldn't follow up any new leads when she was stuck in so many shows. They were pretty much back to back.

Camille's eyes followed her as she shuffled to the changing room. It didn't take a genius to figure out that she was Nathan's plant. Camille was hardly subtle; she'd barely let her out of her sight all morning. Jessica crossed her hands as assistants lifted the dress over her head. She shrugged on a white robe and fastened the belt tightly. She went to get her clothes from the rail but Sara stepped in her way.

"I'd like my ciggies back," she said tightly.

Sara was trying to give up smoking and had asked Jessica to hide a packet in her handbag that morning, before Jessica had seriously annoyed her by landing so many shows. Sara was only walking for Alexander McQueen.

"No. I'm doing you a favour," Jessica said. "It's a filthy habit and you know it."

Sara glared at her, crossing her arms. Even when she frowned, she was stunning, with spiky black hair and amethyst eyes that blazed with anger.

"Jessica's right," Margurita murmured. "Smoking's a terrible idea, Sara, particularly for a model. It'll age your skin. Why jeopardize your chances now that the famous five are out of the picture? I'm certainly not going to."

Sara spun around. "You know them?"

"We belonged to the same agency, but they never had anything to do with me." Margurita shook her long, dark mane. "Not even at the Emerald Ball."

She'd captured Jessica's interest now. "You were there? I saw the photos. It looked amazing."

"It was," Margurita said dreamily. "The hottest men in Hollywood turned up. I had two great snogs."

"What about the famous five?" Sara asked. "How many snogs did they have?"

Margurita snorted. "I wouldn't know. They stayed behind a VIP cordon, drinking magnums of Cristal all night. They even had assistants who kept everyone away. They only let a chosen few get through if the girls thought they were famous enough to speak to. People were actually queuing up, asking for permission to meet them. Tyler thought it was hilarious and tried to sneak in a few 'civilians', but she got caught."

"No way!" Sara said. "I can't wait till I'm famous and can make people queue up to talk to me in clubs. It would be *too* cool."

Jessica rolled her eyes. Sara was soooo shallow.

"Well, people aren't queuing up to see them now," Margurita said cattily.

"What do you mean?" Jessica demanded.

Margurita looked over her shoulder at the assistants who were arranging gowns on a rail. She turned back to Jessica. "They're apparently holed up at some private facility in Switzerland, getting treatment at the agency's expense."

"Treatment for what?"

"No one really knows," Margurita said as she pulled her false eyelashes off. Her voice dropped to a whisper. "But the rumour doing the rounds is they all had plastic surgery that went horribly wrong. Like Frankenstein-bad."

"Ohmigod," Sara gasped. "Did they end up with trout pouts? Are they suing their plastic surgeon?"

"No idea," Margurita said calmly. "And I can't say I care. No one else got a look in while they were around. They took all the best jobs. Now they've gone, I've got Couture Week and a bunch of other jobs. In fact, my agency said Jacey, Olinka and Valeriya were the first choices for *this* job."

Sara's mouth dropped. This was news to her. She obviously thought *she* was the first choice. She really didn't like being second best to anyone.

"It's pretty odd, though, don't you think?" Jessica said. "They're all young and perfect already. Tyler's only eighteen so she can't possibly have any wrinkles."

Margurita shrugged. "There's always someone

younger and hotter than you coming up through the ranks. Maybe even Tyler had started to worry she was in danger of being replaced. Who knows what we'd do if we were in the same position?"

"I'm never having plastic surgery," Sara said with a shudder. "Anyway, some of these young models aren't as hot as they think."

She shot a pointed look at Jessica; she was five years younger than Sara and a lot less experienced at modelling. Jessica ignored her. She quickly removed all traces of the heavy, theatrical make-up, dropping ball after ball of cotton wool into the bin. She pulled on a vintage cream lace blouse she'd discovered at London's Portobello Market and teamed it with black skinny jeans, a Religion black leather jacket and biker boots. She grabbed her bag and was about to make a run for it when Camille tapped the door and peered round.

"Going somewhere I should know about?" She raised an eyebrow.

"No," Jessica said. "I just thought I might do a coffee run."

"Don't worry about it, I'll go in a minute. There's no rush, is there? I thought we could all grab some lunch together but Sara's not even dressed yet."

Jessica forced a smile. She could feel the rein tightening around her.

"You both did brilliantly this morning," Camille said brightly. "I can't wait to see the spread."

"Me too," Sara said, pulling on a black sweater and leggings. "Is there any news about this afternoon? I'm totally psyched."

Camille reddened. "Sorry, Sara. Don't shoot the messenger but head office says there's been a change of plan. You don't need to go to AKSC any more. But hey, you could go shopping instead."

"What are you talking about?" Frowning hard, Sara stalked up to Camille and planted herself, hands on hips, in front of her. "I've practically got this job in the bag. It's my third callback. I have to go."

"Apparently, the client's changed their mind. I'm really sorry but they want to see Jessica instead."

Yes! Margaret must have worked some magic.

"What?" Sara shouted. "You have to be kidding. AKSC's my job, not hers. You can't let her steal it from me."

"She's not stealing it," Camille said calmly. "You

need to stay professional about this. It's not personal. Allegra was passed some pictures from Jessica's shoot in *Teen Mode* and heard about her work for *Mademoiselle*. She thinks she could be perfect for her new project and wants to meet her."

"Unbelievable!" Sara fumed. "That's what she said about me!"

Camille ignored her and walked up to Jessica. "It's up to you, but think of the international exposure you'll get if you're signed by a skincare company like AKSC."

No way could she give up this chance to snoop just to appease a stroppy model. She turned towards Sara. "I'm sorry, but I can't let this opportunity slip through my fingers. I hope you understand that."

"I understand perfectly well," Sara snarled. "You're a little back-stabber, but from now on you should watch *your* back while I'm around." She pushed over a rail of clothes and stomped out of the room.

"*Zut alors!*" an assistant cried. She leapt forward to try and rescue the gowns before they were damaged.

"You did the right thing," Camille said, sighing.

"Sara will get over it in time. Other things will come up for her, but this is your moment. You have to grab it."

"I know," Jessica said.

This casting was her most important to date. It could help her track down Dad.

CHAPTER
THIRTEEN

Photos of Allegra Knight stared down from every inch of the white walls. It was easy to see how she'd once ruled the modelling world. Her long, tanned limbs stretched for ever, while her fine-boned features were perfectly proportioned. She had dark blue eyes, long, glossy blonde hair and a perfect figure. She was undeniably gorgeous, with the extra "something" photographers always looked for.

She'd said she wanted to meet Jessica alone, so Camille had agreed to wait for her back at the hotel. *Even better*. She'd finally shaken her off. She'd checked Allegra out on her iPad in the taxi. She'd become a virtual recluse after quitting modelling when a new wave of supermodels arrived on the scene. Even now, as founder and president of AKSC, she still chose to keep a low profile. Her public appearances were practically non-existent.

Jessica waited for her in a large fifth-floor conference room. This was where Miss Knight conducted all her business meetings, the beautiful brunette who'd escorted her up from reception had explained in hushed tones. A large platter of exotic fruit sat in the middle of the polished oak table, next to trays of pastries, muffins and croissants. Jessica suspected Allegra never touched *those*.

"So you're the young upstart who wants to steal my crown," a voice drawled.

Allegra Knight struck a pose in the doorway with her hands on her hips as if she expected her picture to be taken. She certainly knew how to make an entrance. She wore large black sunglasses emblazoned with "Dior"; a cream wool suit, which looked like Chanel; and Manolo Blahnik stilettos. A camel-coloured silk Hermès scarf was tied around her gazelle-like neck with a flourish. Her hair was still blonde and glossy, skimming her shoulders, and she was perfectly made up. Her face was practically flawless, which made it hard to guess her age. She could be anything between thirty and sixty. This "ageless" look was only obtained with *a lot* of plastic surgery. She must have had a nose job, a facelift and collagen fillers in her cheeks and lips. *At least.*

Jessica picked her nail behind her back. Allegra looked high-maintenance; she'd need a lot of buttering up. "I don't want your crown. I mean, you're a total legend. I couldn't ever compete with that sort of thing."

"Nonsense. Of course you could – and should." Allegra's tone was pleasant. "This isn't a popularity contest, it's modelling. You'll have to get used to stabbing people in the back if you want to succeed in such a snake pit. I'm sure Sara realizes that above anyone else."

Jessica flushed. She flicked her hair over her shoulder. "I didn't—"

"Quiet, please," she said, clicking her fingers. "You're competitive. You made sure that your PA slipped me your portfolio even though the castings had finished. That's nothing to be ashamed of. I like determination in a model. Sara was too predictable, but your beauty intrigues me."

"Thank you. But, honestly, it's all down to my agency, not me." Or rather, it was thanks to Margaret, her "PA".

"False modesty won't get you anywhere in this business or with me, Jessica," she replied. "You should enjoy your beauty while you can, because believe me, it doesn't last. Think about how to bring out your full potential – how you style your hair, make up your face, the way you dress."

Jessica felt her cheeks turn scarlet. Even though Allegra's eyes were hidden behind giant sunglasses, she sensed they were unashamedly roaming over her whole body from head to toe. She felt seriously underdressed next to Allegra's expensive designer labels. She wished she'd worn something else. She hid her hands behind her back again. She was sure Allegra had noticed her other crime against fashion – bitten fingernails.

"Of course, I will. I mean—"

"Because if you're representing my company, you're also representing me, and I expect certain standards," she interrupted. "I dislike the shabby look you young girls seem to favour nowadays. I abhor jeans and flat shoes of any kind, particularly biker boots. I'm looking for elegant swans, not scarecrows."

Allegra wrinkled her nose as she stared at Jessica's feet.

Ouch. She'd never been called a scarecrow before.

"As such I demand a uniform – loose hair worn over the shoulders, a simple but elegant dress, maybe Miu Miu, Christian Dior or Marc Jacobs, and high heels at all times. Will that be a problem for you?"

"No," Jessica lied. She hated high heels. They made her freakishly tall.

"Good. Now come here." Allegra clicked her fingers again.

Jessica blinked. Did she really just do that? She couldn't stand the way clients treated her sometimes. They were *so* rude. She inhaled a mixture of expensive perfume, body lotions and hair products as she drew closer. She also noticed Allegra had a still quality about her. It was unnerving. Her voice sounded impatient yet her face didn't move. There wasn't even a flicker of emotion or a frown.

Allegra grabbed hold of Jessica's chin and moved it from side to side, peering closely at her through her sunglasses as if she were examining some exotic insect under a microscope.

"Times certainly have changed. In my day, imperfections like yours would never have been overlooked. They'd have been seen as ugly. Now, it appears they're all the rage. Freckles, even. Astonishing."

Jessica flushed with anger. She knew she had to be thick-skinned to be a model, as girls were criticized all the time for being too tall, too short, too skinny or too fat. She'd once been told her hair was too "naturally blonde" and her legs were too long, but Allegra had *so* crossed the line. She pulled away. As she took a step back, Allegra's lips attempted to curl into a smirk.

That was why she looked so odd! As well as all the plastic surgery, she'd been Botoxed to within an inch of her life. Her face was completely paralysed. Why did older women think Botox was such a great idea? It didn't make them look younger. Anyway, this frozen freak wouldn't be giving her a job any time soon. That was clear.

"I'm sorry I'm not what you're looking for," she said. She truly was. She hadn't managed to pump her for info yet.

"What makes you say that?" Allegra's lips moved awkwardly into the smallest of smiles. "I think you're perfect in a flawed way. Teenagers around the world will identify with your imperfections and your self-consciousness. I'd reached my decision before you arrived. I'm impressed with your portfolio and think you have potential to become the next big supermodel. I've chosen you to be the face and spokesperson of Teenosity, my revolutionary new face cream for teenage skin. That's if you want the job, of course."

The sunglasses stared blankly at her, throwing down an unknown gauntlet.

"Well?"

"I'd love the job." This was beyond brilliant. She'd thought Allegra hated her looks. Being called an ugly scarecrow hadn't been a great start, but now she'd found her "in". She just had to find a good opportunity to bring up her dad or engineer a detour via the personnel department to dig for stuff on Sam.

"Good. We need to get to work straight away. Legal will draw up a contract and email it to Primus by this evening. The shoot will be on Friday and you'll be contracted to appear at a press launch at the Eiffel

149

Tower the next morning. It'll be broadcast live in fashion stores across Europe before they start to sell my fabulous face cream."

"How's that possible?"

Jessica hadn't been in the industry long, but even she knew it was rare to have the launch of a new product one day after a shoot. Most companies had run-ins of at least six months to a year. How was Allegra going to turn everything around so fast by Saturday? It couldn't be done.

Allegra sensed her scepticism. "It's not usual but it is possible. We wanted a groundbreaking publicity campaign to match the uniqueness of our product. You must have seen our billboards around Paris? Everyone's talking about Teenosity without even knowing what it is."

"That's true. I couldn't work out what the billboard was advertising. It did make me think about it afterwards."

"Exactly," Allegra said. "We'll generate even more interest when the press see a tantalizing glimpse from the shoot and get to meet you in person on Saturday. Once that's started, we'll launch social-media campaigns on Monday morning, extend our billboards across Europe and blitz the fashion glossies. We'll also start distribution in America and the rest of the world. You'll be a huge international star, thanks to me."

Her tone was suddenly surly, as if she somehow resented making the offer. "Well, what do you say for yourself?"

"Thank you. It's just, I . . . I guess I'm surprised. But pleased."

Allegra nodded, her sunglasses fixed on her. "You should be ecstatic. You've done extremely well."

She extended her hand like the Queen. Jessica wasn't sure what to do. Did she expect her to kiss it? She had to be kidding. Jessica settled for a brisk, firm handshake. As she stared down, she noticed Allegra's hands were threaded with blue veins. They seemed to be the only part of her body that had escaped plastic surgery and they gave her age away. She had to be in her sixties. Allegra snatched her hand back as if she'd been slapped

"You may leave now," she said. "I'll make sure you get the details about Friday's shoot."

No! It was too soon. She had to stall. "Please can I have a tour of your labs before I go?"

"Why on earth would you want to do that?" Allegra sounded taken aback but her face was still rigid.

Jessica racked her brains. "Chemistry's one of my favourite subjects at school. It would be great to get an idea of what a real-life lab looks like. I think it'd be helpful to understand how you make the face cream."

Allegra hesitated. It had clearly never dawned on her that a girl could be interested in anything other than modelling. This was probably another black mark against her, along with her freckles, bitten nails and unfeminine biker boots.

"Of course. You shall see where my miracle cream was created. Please wait here while I arrange a tour." She sashayed out of the room, regal-like, leaving behind a cloud of perfume.

Victory! It was time for serious snooping.

CHAPTER FOURTEEN

Half an hour later, Jessica stood shivering in the lab's clean room. A blast of cold air jetted out of the ceiling, chilling her whole body, before being sucked out through the grated floor. No wonder Allegra hadn't wanted to carry out the tour herself. This would mess up her perfect hair. She'd left the honours to her assistant, Lyndon Rawling, a large bear-like American who sported a hair and beard net. He explained the room got rid of tiny particles such as dust from her clothes, which could contaminate the lab. She climbed into a disposable white overall alongside him. Now she too looked like the Abominable Snowman.

The door slid open and she followed him into the lab, a large white room lined with benches, fume cupboards and gloveboxes. A couple of technicians who wore white overalls and safety glasses worked in front of her. Their hands were stuck into gloves which reached inside a large box. She'd learnt at school this was the best way to carry out experiments because it avoided any cross contamination. Chemistry was one of her favourite subjects – that and English literature.

"The lab follows strict health and safety practices," Lyndon said. "We have one entrance in and one exit out, with clean rooms attached to each."

She trailed after him and noticed Allegra watching through the large window. Jessica could still feel her searing gaze as she followed Lyndon across the lab.

"Miss Knight likes to run a tight ship in here," he said. "No personal belongings are allowed. We have a maximum of eight people working in here at any one time to minimize the risk of accidents."

"What's through there?" She spotted another doorway and walked to the back of the lab. It wasn't the exit. She'd already made a point of looking for it in case they had to get out in a hurry. This doorway had a sign saying: DISPOSE OF CONTAMINATED OVERALLS AFTER USE.

"It's just a store cupboard." Lyndon's tone was sharp. "Let me show you something over here, I'm sure you'll find it fascinating."

He pressed his hand into the small of her back, steering her towards a row of microscopes that were lined up next to a series of chemical storage units.

"These are electron microscopes," he said. "We use them to study nanoparticles. They're the only microscopes you can use to see something so small."

She was immediately interested. This was Sam Bishop's line of work.

"Can I?"

"Be my guest."

She put her eye to the microscope. It was extraordinary.

"This is what you're looking at," he said, handing her a vial of liquid. "These are the nanoparticles used in sunblock."

She stared at the liquid and back at the cell under the microscope. It was incredible. The nanoparticles were completely invisible to the human eye. She hadn't seen anything like them in class.

"How can you work with something so small?" Jessica asked.

"We keep the nanoparticles suspended in a liquid solution," he said. "It allows us to manipulate them as and when we need them. We use the zinc oxide nanoparticles in sunblock to reflect UVA and UVB rays, but nanoparticles can be used for almost anything nowadays."

"Have you used these nanoparticles in Teenosity?"

His eyes darted to Allegra, who was still watching through the glass.

"Yes," he said cautiously, "the advances in nanotechnology are amazing. The beauty market hasn't seen anything like it before."

"Why? What's so great about it?"

Come on! He was being *so* cagey. She needed him to open up more. That way she could steer the conversation round to Sam and his nano work.

"It's top secret," he said.

"But I'm supposed to be representing the cream," she protested. "I'll need to know what makes Teenosity so different from other beauty creams if I have to answer questions about it on Saturday."

He looked over his shoulder again. She turned around in time to see Allegra give a small nod. There must be microphones in the lab. She was listening in.

"Teenosity does what no other cream has ever been able to promise before. It can actually halt time," he said.

"That's impossible!"

"Nanotechnology makes it possible. We've created tiny nanorobots that penetrate the skin and target the layer of cells responsible for ageing."

"Nanorobots," she repeated. These were the science-fiction-like creations that Sam had given his lecture about in the States.

"You've heard of them?" Lyndon looked surprised. "Most people think they're children's toys."

"I'm interested in science. I read that nanorobots are minuscule and can be programmed to do whatever you want them to do."

"Exactly. We've programmed our nanorobots to not only delay the ageing process, but to stop it completely."

"No way!"

Lyndon nodded gravely. "It's a miracle."

"So does this mean that teenagers will never age?"

"Their skin won't age," he replied. "Your skin and that of your friends will remain youthful for ever if you continue to use the cream regularly."

She turned to stare at Allegra. She could see why she might resent an upstart like herself. Teenosity had arrived too late to stop her own skin from ageing. It would also help millions of teenagers stay looking younger and more beautiful than her in future. That was enough to get on the nerves of any supermodel, past or present.

"Was Sam Bishop working on Teenosity?" she said.

Crash! A test tube smashed, spilling liquid on to the floor next to the fume cupboards.

A small, balding assistant glanced fearfully across at Lyndon. "I'm sorry," he said, kneeling down. "The test tube caught on my glove. It was an accident."

"Clean it up quickly," he ordered. "We can't afford mistakes like this so close to launch date."

Lab assistants abandoned their posts to mop up the spillage. As one brushed past, his security pass fell off on to the counter. Lyndon was too busy staring at the mess on the floor to notice. So was Allegra – she stood, transfixed, at the window. Jessica stepped forward, pretending to lean on the counter, and scooped it up. This could be useful at some point.

"Thanks, Mr Tarasaki," she muttered under her breath.

"We must leave now," Lyndon snapped. "Follow me."

He marched her through the exit into another clean room. Jessica kept the pass in her clenched fist. She was ready for the blast of air this time and stood still. Lyndon glowered at her. He whipped off his overalls and signalled for her to do the same. She shoved the pass into her jeans pocket as she climbed out of her protective gear. As she looked down, she noticed something stuck in the vent in the floor. She pretended to drop her overalls, managing to tear the object out before he helped her to her feet.

Allegra was waiting outside. Her face was masklike but her voice was low and hard. "Why are you asking about Sam Bishop? Did a newspaper pay you to ask questions? Tell me now!"

Jessica took a deep breath. "I'm sorry. I wanted to know because my dad was looking for him and now he's missing too."

Allegra remained expressionless. "Your father? Whom may I enquire is that?"

"Jack Cole."

"The name sounds familiar. Lyndon?"

He gave a curt nod. "Mr Cole's a private detective. He was hired by Sam Bishop's mother to look for him. British police officers have visited us and we've answered all their questions."

"Cole is a very common name," Allegra said softly. "What a coincidence. I had no idea you were related to him. So many people go missing in Paris each year. Sam and now your father. It's a tragedy."

"Thank you," Jessica said, "but I'm sure I'll find him. In fact, I saw in his diary that he was due to come here on Saturday. Did you meet him?"

The diary was a lie but it didn't seem a good idea to tell her she'd been probing his phone records.

Allegra glanced at Lyndon. "I believe Mr Cole made an appointment."

"But he didn't keep it," Lyndon finished.

"So you never saw him?"

"That's correct," Allegra said. "My office left a message on his voicemail to rearrange but never heard back. We were quite happy to meet with him and discuss Mrs Bishop's concerns. We treat our employees like family here."

Dad had made a call from inside this building on Saturday morning. Why weren't they telling the truth? What were they hiding?

"I'm slightly worried," Allegra said, without a single frown mark appearing. "This must be a very stressful time for you, Jessica, and also a terrible distraction. Did I make a mistake in awarding you this contract when you have so much on your mind? Should I reconsider?"

"No, definitely not," Jessica said. "I'm a professional."

"I'm glad to hear it," Allegra said drily. "In which case, I need you to keep your private life separate from your work. I can't afford to employ a model who's more interested in asking questions than concentrating on the job in hand. We have so much to do and so little time."

"I won't let you down," Jessica said. "You've

answered everything I need to know, thank you. I'll leave the rest to the police. They're the experts."

As if.

Allegra's face relaxed a little but it was hard to tell when she'd had so much Botox. "Good. I know you have a busy schedule so I won't keep you. Don't be late for the shoot. I hate tardiness."

Lyndon led her down the corridor.

"*Bonne chance*," Allegra called after her.

Jessica didn't look back. Her mind was whirring as she followed Lyndon through the labyrinth of corridors to reception. She thanked him and burst through the doors, grateful for the blast of cold air. She didn't stop walking until she was out of sight of the building's CCTV cameras. Then she slowly opened her fist. Lying in her palm was a tiny, exquisite paper swan, identical to the one she'd found in the hotel room. It was the handiwork of Sam Bishop.

A hand roughly grabbed her arm. "What the hell are you doing here?"

She spun around, fist clenched. "Get off me." She yanked her arm away. "This isn't what you think."

"What is it, then?" Nathan fumed. "I warned you

not to interfere and you've gone blundering in there asking about your dad and Sam Bishop!" His grey eyes flashed with anger.

"I didn't blunder in, thanks very much. Allegra Knight invited me here because she wants to employ me."

"She wants to do what?" Nathan looked flabbergasted.

"She's hired me as the face of her new cream for teenagers."

He blanched. "You need to tell me everything that went on in there, and don't you dare leave anything out."

He frogmarched her to a nearby car and threw open the passenger door. She noticed a long-lens camera on the driver's seat. He'd been spying on the building. As he drove away, she reluctantly filled him in on how Allegra had contacted her agency, the tour of the labs, their use of nanotechnology and her modelling deal.

"You're to ring your agency back and tell them to decline the contract," Nathan ordered.

"Not until you investigate Allegra Knight properly."

"Excuse me?" He swerved in front of a car. Heart

beating rapidly, Jessica gripped the door handle tightly as he pulled over. The other driver hooted and gesticulated wildly out of the window.

"Are you actually telling me how to do my job?" he snarled.

Jessica hadn't realized she was holding her breath. She nodded. "As a matter of fact, I am. My dad's life is at stake here. He hasn't got his meds with him. He's going to become ill if I don't find him soon, and you're not doing nearly enough."

Nathan drummed his fingers loudly on the wheel. "I understand your concern, but as I've warned you already, this is far too risky for you to get mixed up in. We're re-interviewing Allegra Knight and I can assure you she's cooperating fully."

"It's funny because that's not how Margaret sees it. She said that Allegra hasn't been exactly forthcoming with either of you."

"You've been speaking to Margaret about this?" His tone was outraged.

"The other night, when you couldn't make it to dinner."

Nathan looked as though he were about to lose it

big time. He might actually explode. He took a deep breath to compose himself. "What, may I ask, did the pair of you decide at this dinner?"

Jessica met his gaze. "That I should try for a casting and see if I could dig anything up at AKSC."

"But—"

"And before you go on, I did pretty well. I found out that Allegra's lying about everything. She claimed my dad had never been to AKSC but his phone records show he made a call from there to Lara Hopkins on Saturday morning. Plus, Allegra's gone along with the reports that Sam's been missing since October, yet he must have been in the building fairly recently because of this."

She produced the tiny origami swan as they waited at a red light.

"This belongs to Sam. I found it in the vents in the lab's clean room. It wouldn't have lasted long in there before being swept away."

Nathan examined the swan curiously. "How do you know it belongs to Sam?"

"Because it's identical to the one I found in his hotel room."

Nathan's face turned beetroot. "That's it! I'm going

to put you on the train back to London myself. We're going to the station right now."

Jessica unbuckled her strap. She reached for the door handle again. "If you do that, I'm going straight to the newspapers. I'll tell them that MI6 is deliberately fitting up an innocent man and ignoring all the evidence that points to AKSC being involved in some kind of cover-up."

Nathan glared back at her. He gripped the steering wheel, his knuckles whitened and jaw clenched.

"I'll do it," Jessica added. "Believe me."

"Unfortunately, I do believe you," he said harshly. "But let's get something straight, Jessica. Playing spy games in your spare time doesn't actually make you a spy. Did you ever consider that your dad could have made a call from the AKSC reception without actually going in to see Allegra? Perhaps he changed his mind or got called away. It's possible. And did it ever cross your mind that someone else dropped one of Sam's swans in the building recently? Perhaps he made one for a work colleague."

Jessica flushed. She hated to admit it, but she hadn't considered any of these alternatives.

"MI6 needs hard evidence before it acts," he continued. "We can't just interrogate someone on the hunches of a headstrong teenager who jumps to conclusions too quickly and is simply incapable of doing what she's told."

"But I—"

"Enough! I'm going to drop you back at your hotel before reporting you to Mrs T. She can decide what action she wants to take against you for deliberately and wilfully disobeying my orders."

"And Allegra?"

"I promise you, we'll look into her closely," he said tersely. "Your father made me your Code Red contact, remember? He trusted me. You need to start trusting me to do my job too."

Jessica glanced out of the window as Nathan pulled out in front of another furious taxi driver. He was, like, the worst driver *ever*. Her dad's decision still made no sense whatsoever. Why would he trust him? Why should she?

"Of course, Nathan," she said mechanically. "As Margaret said the other night, we're all on the same team."

Nathan shot her a puzzled look as she shoved her hand into her jeans pocket. Her fingers touched the pass she'd stolen from the lab. There were some secrets she wasn't prepared to give up, even to her Code Red contact.

CHAPTER

FIFTEEN

Jessica yawned and swayed on her feet as she was stitched into her gown. Last night, she'd had rehearsals for Saint Laurent, Chanel and Alexander McQueen until one a.m. She'd managed to grab a few hours' sleep before she was back again at five a.m. having fittings, make-up and hair tests for all three designers ahead of the day's shows. Haute Couture Week was exhausting. It was hardly surprising the make-up artists had to slap lots of under-eye concealer on all the models. Everyone looked shattered.

It was ten a.m. and she'd already been sewn into an exquisite green floor-length gown with a long train and a traffic-stopping ruffled red dress with a huge corsage at Saint Laurent. Her line-up at Chanel included a jewel-encrusted silver lace gown with layers of hand-beaded tulle and a shimmering white sequinned creation. Seamstresses had checked all the dresses fitted perfectly and taken Polaroids of her wearing each outfit. They stuck the pictures to the clothes hangers to help assistants remember who was wearing which gown during the frantic mid-show outfit changes.

Now she was at Alexander McQueen: her final fitting. She closed her eyes as she stood in front of the mirror. What were Margaret and Nathan up to? She hadn't heard a peep out of either of them despite leaving messages on both their mobiles. Had they re-interviewed Allegra?

"Stop slouching, *s'il vous plait*," a seamstress said.

She straightened up. Apart from the short taxi rides between the couture houses earlier, she'd been standing in front of mirrors or practising walking for the last four hours. She longed to escape. This fitting was dragging on for ever as the stylists experimented with different ways of doing her hair while Camille watched, hawklike.

"You look amazing," she said, peering over her shoulder.

Jessica looked up and gaped at her astonishing

appearance in the full-length mirror. A gothic princess stared back. She was squeezed into a royal blue boned corset that produced a tiny eighteen-inch waist. The blue silk skirt had a massive train, which was so heavy it felt like she was dragging a small child after her, and her rose gold stilettos had the most vertiginous heels she'd ever tried on. She resembled a skyscraper, standing at almost seven feet tall.

Hairstylists busied themselves around her. They'd decided on a massive beehive, which would be studded with Cartier diamond clips tonight, making her look even taller. A woman stood on a chair and perched a gold crown precariously on the top of her bird's nest hair.

"Voila!"

The whole effect was amazing yet bizarre.

"Wow!" Camille stared admiringly at her.

Jessica tried to turn around and lost her balance, almost toppling over the seamstresses who knelt at her feet, pinning the hem.

"I can't get used to wearing these heels," she groaned. "They're too high and a size too big. I know I'm going to land flat on my face on the catwalk."

"You'll be fine," Camille said. "You need to keep your eyes fixed straight ahead as you come down the runway. Don't worry. I'll be there tonight and I'll keep an eye out for you."

Jessica sighed. *Of course she would.*

She had a few hours to spare before the first show. Camille had accompanied her back to her hotel room, but Jessica had fled minutes later and flagged down a taxi in the street without being caught. She made the driver take a detour past AKSC, hoping to catch a glimpse of Nathan's car, but the street was empty. She hesitated as the taxi pulled up outside. She had the key card in her bag. It was tempting to blag her way in but it was too risky. She'd probably get caught, then sacked, and maybe even arrested. She'd certainly be packed off back to London. She had to find out what Nathan and Margaret were doing now that she'd managed to shake off the limpet.

She fished out the card Nathan had given her. Margaret hadn't told her where she was staying, but she was probably at the Ritz too. She checked her emails and surfed websites until they arrived at 15

Place Vendôme. She paid the driver and jumped out. The hotel was as breathtaking as she'd expected, with gleaming marble floors and glittering chandeliers. It was also busy enough for her to blend in without drawing too much attention to herself.

She marched straight past the front desk and up the massive red-carpeted staircase to the second floor. Nathan had helpfully given her his room number: 222. She knocked on the door. No answer. Even better. She looked up and down the corridor for the housekeeping trolley. He might have left some useful documents lying about. She went in search of a maid and found her in a nearby suite. She explained in French that it was her dad's room. The maid smiled and swiped her in before she could even pretend to be locked out.

That was frighteningly easy.

The suite was huge and decorated in soft green pastel tones, with gold fittings and a luxurious carpet that had to be Persian. It was so soft, her feet sank into it. She spotted Nathan's laptop on the large ornate oak desk and walked over to check it out. It was switched off and she knew it was pointless to try and guess his passwords. She'd need to be a super hacker to get into an MI6 laptop.

His gun and passport lay next to it, on top of a pile of interior design magazines. She examined the passport. Talk about grim-faced. Anyone would think he was standing in front of a firing squad.

Cheer up, Nathan. Working for Mrs T couldn't be that bad.

Then again, it probably was.

Her foot nudged something under the desk. She fished out a battered brown leather briefcase. The gold clasp was open. Delving inside, she pulled out a sheaf of files. They were all stamped MI6 CONFIDENTIAL. She flicked through them. One contained a list of Algerian agents. She also found the file of French agents and Vectra's photos. That was odd. These were the files she'd discovered on the floor of her dad's study. But why did Nathan have them?

Her mouth fell open as she stared at the images in another file. They were of her – taken with a long-lens camera as she travelled to her underwater modelling shoot in east London. Here she was again after the shoot, running from the bus stop to school.

She remembered the camera in Nathan's car when he'd intercepted her outside the AKSC building. Why had he been spying on her on Monday morning? She shivered. It was creepy to think he'd been watching her every move without her even realizing it. What was his game?

She went through the rest of the briefcase but there wasn't anything useful. She opened the top left desk drawer and pulled out a plastic bag. Inside was a pink, crystal mobile phone and a backstage pass for Haute Couture Week marked Lara Hopkins. She examined the phone through the plastic. On the back, crystals formed the letter "L" for Lara. Luckily it was turned off; otherwise Nathan could have picked up when she'd tried ringing it a couple of days ago.

Her heart raced as she fished out a brown wallet from the other drawer. Quickly, she checked the credit cards. It was definitely Nathan's. But why didn't he have it with him? Maybe he'd just popped down to reception, which meant she probably didn't have much time before he returned. She went through the wallet. Tucked in the back pouch was a piece of folded, dog-eared paper.

She gasped as she smoothed it out. It was another picture of her, except this time it wasn't taken with a long lens. It was a family shot. She balanced on one leg at her mum and dad's feet, wearing a floppy pink hat and sundress. She looked about four. It must have been taken shortly before her mum's death. She touched her pendant. Mum wore it around her neck in the photo. The picture looked like it had been well-thumbed; both her mum and dad's faces had faded beneath white crease marks, giving them a ghostly appearance, while she grinned brightly.

This was beyond creepy. Why was he so interested in her family? Why was he collecting photos of *her*?

Jessica froze. A muffled voice drifted out from behind a door on the far side of the room. Her eyes darted around, taking in the clues. She'd been distracted by its sheer opulence. Now she noticed the shoes on the floor. His jacket, gun and wallet were here too. Why hadn't she figured it out already? Nathan hadn't gone anywhere. He must still be in the suite. She stuffed the picture back into the wallet and threw it in the drawer. She shoved the briefcase under the desk before creeping to the bedroom door, which was ajar. She couldn't see him through the gap. She pushed the door open wider and caught her breath. He was on his mobile in the en suite marble bathroom.

"I'm telling you, she's guessed where her dad is and she could blow this whole thing wide open if we're not careful. We can't let that happen." He listened intently while the other person spoke for a few seconds. "So Lily and Jack were expendable and now Jessica is? Right?" He spat the words out angrily.

A shiver passed down her back. Who was he talking to and why were they discussing Mum? Why were they talking about *her* as if she were a piece of worthless rubbish about to be thrown away?

"I disagree," Nathan continued. "We need to get rid of Jessica. Surely you can see that? She's getting in the way. I can be with her in 20 minutes and end this thing right now."

She crept back through the room, quietly closed the suite door behind her and fled down the corridor to the staircase.

Expendable, expendable, expendable.

The word pounded in her head with every footstep.

We need to get rid of Jessica. She's getting in the way.

When she reached the bottom of the stairs, she stopped and gripped the handrail tightly. Her hands shook with rage. She'd go back to Nathan's room and grab his gun. She'd point it at him and demand to know why he wasn't doing anything about rescuing Dad. She'd ask why he wanted to get rid of her so badly and why he claimed her mum was expendable. She didn't have anything to do with this. What on earth was he talking about?

Somehow they were all expendable to him.

The photos in his file and wallet were *really* worrying. What did he want with her? And why did he have the incriminating files from Dad's study? When he stared down the barrel of a gun, he'd have to tell her the truth. She started back up the stairs again and stopped. She could hear her dad's voice in her head.

A good spy always thinks things through logically, without losing control of their emotions.

He was right, as usual. She had to calm down. It'd be tough, but she couldn't let Nathan suspect she knew

something was up. She had to play along with him if she wanted to find out what was really going on. If she confronted him, he'd deny, deny, deny. He'd been trained to tell lies. It was what he did for a living.

She sat in the foyer waiting for him, her eyes glued to the lift.

The lift door opened and a group of businessmen and an elderly Japanese couple walked out, followed by Nathan. She closed her eyes. She had to put on an act, the way she did when she was modelling. She stopped being Jessica Cole and became a mermaid, a rock chick or a gothic princess in front of the camera. Today, she had to be a naïve, grateful teenager who believed everything she was told.

"Nathan!" she called. "Over here!"

He jumped and gave her a piercing scowl. He barged past a businessman, knocking his newspaper to the marble floor. He thundered towards her without apologizing to the startled man. "What the hell are you doing here?"

"You gave me your hotel card. Remember?" She waved it gaily at him.

He stared back suspiciously. "What's up with you?"

She lost the grin. She had to tone it down. He wasn't used to bright, cheerful Jessica. He'd only met the stroppy, disobedient one so far.

"I had a break before the shows so I thought I'd come and find out if you've looked into Allegra Knight yet," she said loudly.

He grabbed her arm and pulled her roughly to her feet. Now they were back on familiar territory: her challenging everything he said.

"Not here," he snapped.

He held her arm tightly as he led her to the lift and back upstairs to his suite. She followed him inside. He'd tidied his laptop and gun away but the briefcase now sat in its place. She rubbed her arm. It still smarted from where he'd gripped her.

"Have you been in here?" he said abruptly.

"Of course not. Why?" She managed to keep her best poker face. Maybe she'd left the briefcase a fraction of an inch too far to the left or right. He was the kind of person who'd notice if the tiniest detail was out of place.

He scrutinized her. "Never mind. I just don't like being surprised, that's all."

"Really?" Jessica said. "I love surprises. I remember when—"

"I've just got off the phone with Mrs T and she agrees with me," he interrupted. "There's a *slim* possibility that your dad and Sam could be inside AKSC, but we can't go storming in. It would scare Vectra and the *real* Starfish away before they do the pickup. We can't risk that happening. We need to catch both of them red-handed."

She stared at him. It was a plausible enough explanation, but she didn't believe a word he said. Not now she'd seen his secret stash of photos and knew how little her family meant to him.

"What about Dad? Where does he fit into all this?" Her fingers made tight fists. She felt like screaming or hitting him. Or both.

"Apparently that's where you come in. We've tried to get an undercover MI6 agent embedded inside AKSC but the mission's failed and we don't have time to build up new contacts again."

He cracked his knuckles one after another, setting her teeth on edge. Couldn't he give his medieval torture methods a rest?

"This goes against all my better judgements, but Mrs T has been persuaded that you're our best shot at getting into AKSC. She thinks there's a good chance you could be invited back by Allegra after tomorrow's shoot."

"So now you *do* want me to investigate?" She crossed her arms. "After everything you've said; your threats to send me home?"

Nathan instantly jumped down her throat. "Mrs T wants you to do this. Margaret too. I'd send you back home right now if it were left to me. Unfortunately, it's not my call."

Was that what he meant when he said he wanted to get rid of her right now? Or was he referring to something more sinister?

"What does Mrs T want me to do?"

"Just what your father's taught you – be alert and notice your surroundings. Don't do anything that puts you at risk but report back anything that looks out of the ordinary. How does that sound?"

He looked even more annoyed when she didn't reply. "I thought you'd be pleased. What is it with you teenagers? You said you wanted to help, or have you changed your mind? Do you have something better to do?"

"Not at all," she said hastily.

Nathan's eyes burned into her face. "Nerves are good," he said finally, misinterpreting her hesitation. "They mean you're not going to do something rash. This should help too." He handed her a large silver make-up bag. "I can't let you go in there unequipped. This was prepared in advance for our undercover agent. Mrs T agreed you should have it now."

"What's inside? Do I get a gun?"

"Of course not." He looked horrified as she emptied the bag on to the table. Lipsticks and powders spilled out.

"Oh great. More make-up. Like I don't have enough of this stuff already," she said, rolling her eyes.

"This is make-up with a difference. It comes from MI6's gadget department."

Her eyes lit up. This was more like it. Now she could protect herself. Possibly even from him.

"I thought this would get your attention for once," he said drily.

"What does this do?" She picked up a silver powder

compact. It had a large blue stone set in the middle. He whipped it off her.

"Watch and learn. I don't have time to run through it all twice."

He pressed the stone and lifted the lid, aiming it at the wall.

"Wow!" Jessica squinted over his shoulder. She could see straight into the room next door through the compact lid. A man lay on the bed, watching TV and holding a glass. He got up and walked into the bathroom.

"Awesome!"

"The lid has X-ray vision," Nathan explained. "Play around with it, but don't mess with the powder unless you really need it. If you blow it into someone's eyes they'll be temporarily blinded."

He placed it back in the bag before she had chance to try that function out. Maybe he sensed she was sorely tempted to use it on him.

"The blue stone is also removable and contains a mini electromagnetic pulse which disables any electrical device within two metres," Nathan continued. "Make sure you keep it away from your mobile and laptop."

"And this?" She picked up a can of hairspray.

"Careful!" He snatched it off her. "It's a flame-thrower and has a range of three metres."

If only he'd hand it over. He stood right in front of her. She couldn't possibly miss.

"Try this on." He clamped a chunky silver bracelet around her wrist.

Wow. She might actually get to use something.

"Does it detonate in twenty seconds?" She was only half-joking. He could actually be trying to kill her.

"This turns you into Spider-Woman," Nathan said coldly. "You pull the catch here and take aim. It shoots out a tensile wire which attaches to any surface and acts as a safety harness. The compound of carbon nanotubes makes it ten times stronger than steel even though it has the thickness of a piece of thread. It'll carry the weight of at least ten men."

He swiftly undid the bracelet and then ran through the rest of the gadgets. It was mind-blowing stuff. The eyeshadow palette was also a mini computer, which he'd programmed to send emails to a protected MI6 account. A huge emerald ring hid a laser, a lipstick doubled as a torch and a tracking device and a bottle of perfume sprayed a foam solution that expanded and solidified within sixty seconds. It made it useful for copying keys in locks or taking out CCTV cameras. The best part was that after an hour or two the foam melted, leaving no trace that it had ever been there.

She secretly liked the diamond stud the best. She'd got her belly button pierced one Saturday afternoon with Becky but hadn't dared tell her dad or Mattie yet. She knew they'd hit the roof. She turned around and put the stud in straight away before Nathan could take that off her too.

"Hold the stem and turn the stud clockwise until it clicks," Nathan said. "Rubbing the diamond on any surface releases particles which can cut through glass and even steel. We use similar devices in hostage situations."

She pulled her top down and faced him, hands on hips. "I thought you said you didn't want me to do anything risky? It seems like you're equipping me for a mini-war with this arsenal. What's inside AKSC? Is there something you're not telling me?"

His face reddened. "As I said, these gadgets were put together for one of our agents, just to be on the safe side."

"Well, I don't feel particularly safe when you haven't let me try a single one out," Jessica said. "What if I can't remember how they work once I'm inside AKSC?"

"You will. You're bright. But don't worry. You'll probably never need any of these gadgets. I'd just prefer you to have them for my own peace of mind."

She rammed the emerald ring on to her index finger. He sounded like he was genuinely concerned for her safety, but who was he kidding? As if he cared about her. She was expendable, just like Mum and Dad.

"Thanks," she said stiffly, "but I need to shoot off. I've got to get ready for the shows."

"OK, but let's speak again tomorrow after the shoot. Good luck, Jessica, and be careful."

Yeah, right. Like he meant it. What a hypocrite.

CHAPTER
SIXTEEN

"Why does Nathan have a photo of my family in his wallet?"

She'd rung Margaret as soon as she'd left The Ritz and this time she'd picked up after a couple of rings. Jessica stared out of the taxi window, en route to the Musée Rodin for the Alexander McQueen show, waiting for her to reply. She'd been pretty upfront at dinner and she needed someone to be straight with her now.

"Margaret?"

"You're certain?" Margaret was playing for time. She could hear it in her voice.

"I was snooping in his room and found it. I heard

him talking on the phone too. He said Mum and Dad were expendable. Me too. Why was he talking about Mum? What does she have to do with this?"

The phone remained silent.

"Are you still there, Margaret?"

"This is difficult."

"Tell me. I'm not a kid any more." It was seriously annoying the way people treated her like a grown-up one minute and a little girl the next. "I can deal with things, you know, like going into AKSC undercover."

"I realize that, Jessica. How much do you know about your mum?"

Good question. Truthfully, hardly anything. Shutters always came down whenever she asked Mattie or Dad about her.

"Just that she used to be a model. Quite a successful one. She died in a helicopter crash on the way to a shoot in Naples."

Margaret hesitated. "This really shouldn't be coming from me. There must be someone else you can talk to about this. Someone you're close to."

"There isn't." She couldn't possibly ring Mattie without giving the game away about Dad. She'd never get a straight answer out of her anyway. She never did. "Please, Margaret."

Margaret exhaled heavily. "This is going to come as a shock to you, Jessica." She paused. "Your mum was an MI6 agent too."

Jessica leant forward, gripping her phone tightly. "That's not possible. Dad would have told me. She was a model. I've seen the pictures."

"She was a model and a spy. A very good one too."

"If that's true, why didn't Dad tell me? Or Mattie?"

"They were probably trying to protect you."

"Protect me from what, exactly?" Jessica lowered her voice but the driver's music was so loud he couldn't hear anything anyway. None of this made any sense.

"The helicopter crash happened while she was working for MI6. She was on assignment with Nathan."

"What?" Jessica slumped back in her seat. "She worked with *him*?"

"Sometimes. We all worked together back then – your dad, Nathan and me. Your mum was in a different division but we collaborated on certain projects. We were a tight team."

Jessica was speechless. Why had Dad and Mattie kept this from her? What was the big deal? She knew about her dad's espionage past. Didn't they trust her with Mum's secret?

"So I guess that's when Dad made Nathan his Code Red contact, right?" Jessica said.

"He was a natural choice. They were partners and friends. They always had each other's backs." Margaret stopped herself.

"Go on."

She sighed. "Your father and Nathan had a big falling out after your mother's death. Shortly afterwards, your father became ill and went off on extended sick leave. He never returned to MI6."

"What did they fall out about?" Jessica demanded.

"The crash. Nathan was supposed to be on the flight with your mother but he was running late that day and missed it."

"And Dad blamed him? Was it his fault?"

"That's all I'm allowed to say, Jessica. The rest is above my clearance level. All I know is that when

Nathan recently warned your father against coming to Paris, he admitted it was the first time they'd spoken in years."

Jessica took a sharp intake of breath. Code Red must have been a terrible, terrible mistake. Her dad hadn't changed his contact point from back then. He probably never thought he'd need it once he left the service. He couldn't have wanted her to turn to someone he'd fallen out with. Nathan had no loyalty to him either. He believed he was expendable, that her mum was expendable. Her too. She couldn't get the photo in his wallet out of her head.

"You said at dinner that the person who set up my dad could have been someone he's crossed in the past," Jessica said quietly.

Margaret paused. "Yes, I still believe that. This seems very personal."

That's because it was personal. Nathan had conveniently accepted all the fake evidence that had been planted on Dad. He'd tried to keep her out of AKSC until he was overruled. Why? Because her dad was there and he didn't want her to find him. It would ruin his deal with Vectra.

"Could Nathan be Starfish?" she blurted out. "He could have planted all the evidence against Dad and attacked me that day. I know he was following me. He's got photos of me taken with a long-lens camera in his briefcase."

Margaret fell silent again.

"All I can say is this," she said finally. "You need to be extra vigilant. Starfish has killed once already. He could strike again if he thinks you're about to blow his cover."

Camille's mouth was moving rapidly and her arms were waving about but Jessica had no idea what she was saying. She felt totally numb as an assistant laced her into an emerald lace gown an hour later. Her mum was a former MI6 agent who'd lost her life while on the job – a fact both her dad and Mattie had tried to cover up. Her dad held Nathan responsible in some way. Now it was highly likely that his former friend and colleague had turned double agent and set him up.

"I said I'm sorry about November," Camille repeated.

"What?"

Her chaperone was still jabbering away. She nodded at an Amazonian redhead who was being helped into the Alexander McQueen gothic princess gown Jessica had been fitted for that morning. A stylist laced up the boned corset as November held her breath.

"McQueen's team decided at the last minute to go with November because she's got more experience of opening shows," Camille said. "It's outrageous. I've been arguing with them for the last half hour but I can't get them to change their minds. I'm going to have another go at them right now."

"Don't bother," Jessica said. "I don't care."

"Sure you don't," Sara said, as a make-up artist touched up her crimson lips nearby. "Remember, what goes around comes around."

"Oh do shut up!" Jessica snapped.

"Now girls, play nice," Camille said. "I have to stop this before it's too late and—"

"AAAARGGGH!"

A scream rang out. "Get it off me! Get it off me!" November shrieked. She tore frantically at the dress, ripping the blue silk.

"Stop it!" a seamstress ordered. "You're ruining it!"

"Help me! Someone help!"

November let out a blood-curdling scream and collapsed. Her body jolted and twitched on the floor as frothy saliva bubbled out of her scarlet lips. Seamstresses and stylists stood by helplessly, watching her fit.

Jessica lunged forward and grabbed a pair of scissors from a table. She hacked into the corset, cutting it open.

"Ohmigod."

November's torso was covered in large purplish welts. She looked like she'd fallen victim to the bubonic plague. Jessica ripped the corset off her body and felt her wrist for a pulse. There wasn't one.

"Someone call for an ambulance!" She pumped November's chest with the palms of her hands. She paused for a few seconds and blew into her mouth, watching her chest rise up and down. Then she used her palms again. It felt like an age before she was pushed aside by paramedics. They hooked her up to a monitor and used paddles to shock her heart back to life.

"What's happened to her?" Jessica asked in French. "What's caused these swellings?"

"It looks like she's had a severe allergic reaction to something that stopped her heart," one of the paramedics replied. "Has she drunk anything in the last few minutes? It's possible she's ingested a poison of some kind."

"I've no idea, sorry."

Jessica sat back on her heels and stared at the dress she'd hacked to pieces. Using a pair of scissors, she carefully pulled back the corset. A fine white powder clung to the seams. November hadn't drunk something toxic. The dress had been poisoned.

It wasn't meant for November. Someone was trying to kill Jessica.

She glanced up and noticed Sara staring at her. She'd wanted to exact revenge on her for landing the AKSC job, but this was way beyond her. This was the work of a professional. Margaret had warned her Starfish could come after her. He knew she was getting close. Nathan had to be working with someone who had access to all areas and could get to the dresses without alerting suspicion. She looked about the room. Camille was slumped on the floor in floods of tears. A paramedic placed a blanket around her shoulders.

He didn't realize they were just crocodile tears.

Backstage was sombre as the models got changed back into their "civvie" gear. The show had been cancelled and gendarmes were taking down details of all the models booked to appear. They hadn't figured out yet that the dress was meant for Jessica. She wasn't going to draw attention to herself by telling them.

"I need some powder," a brunette model said. "You don't mind if I borrow yours, do you? I can't find mine." She delved into Jessica's silver make-up bag on the counter without waiting for a reply.

"No! Don't do that." Jessica snatched the compact back. A gendarme looked at her curiously and turned away.

"Sorry! It's only powder, you know!" She rolled her eyes at the other models and stormed off in a huff.

They glared at Jessica and obviously thought she was a complete cow. How could she tell them the truth? The powder wasn't something they'd want anywhere near their faces.

"Oh chill out," Sara said, sipping from a silver hip flask. She lurched towards her and gripped the table. "Everyone's upset about Autumn but she's going to live, so it's OK."

"November," Jessica said. "She's called November."

"Autumn, November, December, whatever," Sara slurred. "Seems a pretty stupid name to me."

Jessica rolled her eyes as she slurped from her flask. She was drunk and would probably only get more offensive as the evening wore on. Sara was about to take another swig when someone ripped it out of her hand.

"No drinking alcohol backstage," Aurelie Leseuer, one of the show's directors, hissed. "Police are crawling all over the place. This doesn't look good for us on top of everything else that's happened."

"Whoops!" Sara giggled as she crashed into a table and almost fell over.

"Where's your chaperone?" Madame Leseuer asked.

"She's gone to hospital for a check-up," Sara said in a sing-song voice. "Hip hip hooray! We're free!"

She punched the air and took a gulp from the flask.

"Perhaps you could take her home," Madame Leseuer said, turning to Jessica, "before she causes any more embarrassment."

Great. She'd learnt bombshell news about her mum, survived an assassination attempt courtesy of Nathan and Camille, and now she was babysitting a drunk. Her day couldn't get any worse.

"OK." She sighed as she scooped up her goodie bag, which was packed with freebies, including make-up and a cream Chanel clutch bag and matching pumps.

"*Bonne*. There's a taxi rank just outside." Madame Leseuer nodded to the door.

Jessica helped Sara through the backstage area, tripping over discarded rose-coloured stilettos. As soon as she was outside, Sara took a few more swigs from her flask.

"Sssorry about that," she slurred, swinging her bag wildly. "And I'm sorry about November. That dress was meant for you, you know. You must be, like, freaked out."

"Yes, I am," Jessica admitted.

"Why do you think someone wants to kill you? Is it because you're, like, really annoying?"

Jessica glared at her. "Yet your dress wasn't poisoned. That's a shocker!"

"Touché!" Sara said, giggling. She froze as she clocked a black stretch limo parked nearby.

"What's the matter now?"

The limo door opened and Lyndon Rawling climbed out. He walked towards them, with a lop-sided grin.

"Jessica, apologies for the last-minute surprise but Miss Knight wants you to be her guest tonight. The shoot's been shifted and she needs you to be available to work from six thirty a.m."

"But I don't have my bags with me," she protested.

"Don't worry. Miss Knight apologizes once more for the inconvenience but she's already arranged for your bags to be transferred from the hotel to her suite. They're there now. It'll save time in the morning if the car can take you straight from AKSC instead of picking you up from your hotel."

Jessica bit her lip. Was this a trap?

"So this is actually a command, not an invite to see the great Allegra Knight?" Sara said, tittering. "I'm glad I didn't get the job after all. Sounds like a total drag when I can go out partying instead."

Lyndon scowled at her and turned back to Jessica. "Miss Knight thought you'd prefer to have your own belongings around you. She also thought you'd be more comfortable with her. Hotels can be so impersonal and, well, distracting."

He stared disapprovingly at Sara, who swayed and clutched Jessica's arm to stop herself from falling over. Then he took in Jessica's slouchy chocolate sweater, jeans and black boots. She wasn't wearing her AKSC uniform. She met his gaze. As if she cared what he thought.

"It's a huge honour that Miss Knight has invited you," Lyndon insisted. "She rarely allows guests into Allegra Towers."

"Probably because it's so dull," Sara said loudly. "It sounds beyond lame, Jessica. Come back to my room and watch TV instead while I crack open the minibar."

Jessica looked from Sara to Lyndon. She sensed danger, yet she couldn't walk away. Not if there was a chance she could find Dad tonight.

"Is there a problem?" Lyndon asked.

"Not at all. I'm, well . . . I guess I'm surprised. It's late and, you know, people will be worried if I don't go back to the hotel."

"We've already reached Camille on her mobile and she's fine about it. You don't have anyone else here with you in Paris we need to speak to, do you?" Lyndon's tone was provocative. He wasn't going to accept a refusal.

"Of course not," she said. "I'm thrilled to be invited. It's a huge honour, thanks."

"No way!" Sara said. "Don't do it, Jessica! It'll be like a total snorefest."

"Excuse me." Lyndon brushed past. He took Jessica's handbag and returned to the limo, placing it in the boot.

Great. Now she didn't have her mobile close to hand.

Lyndon opened the passenger door and climbed in as the driver switched on the engine.

"You don't have to do this," Sara said urgently. She was no longer slurring or swaying on her feet. In fact, she sounded totally sober.

"Yes I do," Jessica said. "You wouldn't understand."

Lyndon peered out and shot a filthy look at Sara. "Are you ready to go, Miss Cole? The driver's waiting."

"Yes." She walked to the door but Sara suddenly lunged at her. She flung her arms around her in a tight bear hug.

"Be very careful," she hissed in her ear.

"What—?"

Sara pushed Jessica away before she could finish her sentence and handed her the flask. "Have a drink on me," she said cheerily. "I insist, for old time's sake."

Jessica hesitated. She undid the lid and took a sip. It was water, not alcohol.

Sara was pretending to be drunk. What was going on?

:CHAPTER:
SEVENTEEN

AKSC looked even more impressive by night. Spotlights lit up the white ten-storey building, accentuating its classic, elegant lines. Jessica clutched her bag tighter as Lyndon guided her through a side door and into a private elevator. Did he already know she was here to spy?

Stop freaking out.

All she had to do was act normal and he wouldn't suspect anything – the way she'd never guessed that there was more to Sara than met the eye. She seemed so shallow and catty and well, er, dumb. But was that all an act too? Could she have been the MI6 agent that Margaret had been trying to get embedded into AKSC all along? It'd explain why Sara had been so furious when Jessica landed the Teenosity job. Losing Allegra's contract had scuppered MI6's undercover operation. Sara had no way of legitimately getting inside AKSC HQ once Teenosity slipped through her fingers, but now Jessica had the perfect cover.

The elevator door pinged open at the top of Allegra Towers, making her jump. She stepped out and followed Lyndon down the corridor. The floor was expensively carpeted in cream wool and the walls were dotted with tasteful black and white photos of Allegra. The woman's vanity knew no bounds. She was absolutely everywhere.

Jessica's eyes rested on the only colour photo, which featured Allegra dripping with diamonds and wearing an off-the-shoulder aquamarine evening gown. She was surrounded by glamorous girls holding glasses of champagne. Allegra clutched a glass of orange juice and smiled enigmatically at the camera. Her eyes widened as she recognized the models in the photograph.

Tyler, Olinka, Jacey, Darice, Valeriya.

The famous five. They were all there. The photo looked familiar. She remembered Darice's slashed Versace dress.

"Miss Knight's particularly fond of this photograph," Lyndon said, observing her interest.

"I've seen a similar photo of the supermodels online," Jessica said slowly. "This must have been taken at Emerald's fiftieth anniversary ball last December."

A look of surprise flickered across Lyndon's face. "Well spotted. Miss Knight doesn't normally enjoy public appearances, but this was one social event she didn't want to miss."

"So why did she attend?"

"She was Emerald's most famous supermodel. She modelled for the agency for more than ten years and landed over a dozen covers of *Vogue*."

Interesting. "I had no idea she was an Emerald model too. Does she know the famous five well? I read they'd all quit modelling."

Lyndon's eyes remained fixed on the photo. "Not at all. Miss Knight had the pleasure of meeting them for the first time that evening. They'd asked to be introduced to her, as she's such an icon."

"Really?"

He guided her along the corridor before she could

quiz him any further. He swiped open a door as if he were in a hotel.

"This is your suite. Miss Knight regrets she isn't able to welcome you in person, as she's retired for the night. She hopes you'll be comfortable here."

"I'm sure I will," she said, stepping inside.

It was huge – far bigger than her hotel room. The walls, carpets, bed, cushions and wardrobes were all white. There wasn't a touch of colour anywhere. She knew it was supposed to look chic and minimalist but instead it felt clinical and impersonal. Yet more black and white photos of Allegra were strategically placed around the room, giving the sense she was watching her at all times. Every surface had vases and vases of lilies and white roses.

She stared at them, distracted by the sudden reminder of her mum.

"If you need anything, don't hesitate to call," Lyndon said. "Just pick up the phone and you'll go straight through to housekeeping. We have a private chef on call throughout the night and a maid who'll get anything else you want."

"Wow. Twenty-four-hour room service. It's like

being back in my hotel, except better, of course. It's beyond cool." She smiled brightly. It was hard to keep up the act, but she had to. She was here for only one reason. Dad.

"There are a few more rules here, for security reasons," Lyndon said. "The doors on this floor, including your own, will automatically lock in precisely five minutes. The lift will also be deactivated."

She gazed at him open-mouthed. "Are you crazy? What if there's an emergency and I need to get out?"

"If there's a fire, an alarm will sound and the security system will be rebooted. This will unlock the doors and the lift. You can leave using the emergency stairs at the end of the corridor. I hope you understand this system is for everyone's safety. It prevents anyone from the labs ever coming up here."

And it stopped anyone getting down to the labs, which looked like an interesting part of the building. Double blast.

"I wish you a good night and sweet dreams." Lyndon smiled, but his eyes were hard.

"Thanks," Jessica said.

"Oh, one final thing." He paused in the doorway.

"The doors will unlock at five thirty a.m. sharp. The breakfast room is the first door on your right. Miss Knight's suite is further along the corridor. She rarely eats breakfast so she'll catch up with you later in the day. She hopes you enjoy your stay and wishes you *bonne chance* at the shoot tomorrow."

Jessica perched on the edge of the bed as he walked out. Sure enough, a few minutes later the door clicked. She tried the handle to make sure but she really had been locked inside. Who – apart from a paranoid control freak – locked their guests in their rooms at night? She was staying with the hostess from hell. She stared at her bags on the bed. She hated the thought of a stranger going through her things and packing them up. It was beyond creepy. Had someone from AKSC done the same thing to Sam?

She had a quick scout around the room but couldn't find any more paper swans: clues he'd stayed there. She texted Mattie to say she was tired after the shows and going to bed and switched off the iPhone. She whipped the stolen pass out of her bag and tried swiping it by the door sensor but it was useless. Either the pass had been disabled or, more likely, the assistant didn't have clearance to be in Allegra Towers. There had to be another way out of here. Sensors were stationed above the door, detecting when it opened and closed, and a smoke alarm was fixed in the centre of the ceiling.

That was it. She dug around in her bag and found the packet of ciggies and lighter she'd confiscated from Sara as well as the cool perfume bottle. She flicked open the lighter beneath the sensor. Immediately, the fire alarm screeched. She didn't have much time before security came to check up on her. The lock clicked. She pushed the door open and ran out. She'd already spotted the camera on the wall as she'd walked past. To her surprise, a single spray of perfume took it out. She'd half expected some of Nathan's gadgets to be fakes. A blob of foam appeared and expanded, covering the camera in seconds. She took out a second camera and darted back along the corridor. Just as she reached her door, the lift opened. She sprayed the lock and managed to light a cigarette and take a quick puff before someone banged on the door.

"Miss Cole? Is everything OK in there?"

"Yes, thanks!"

Lyndon strode in, red-faced and sweating. He looked like he'd been running.

She tried her best to look sheepish, dangling a cigarette between her fingers. She wasn't acting when she coughed. God, it tasted gross.

"I'm sorry," she said, choking. "Is this because of me?" She waved the cigarette in the air.

"I should have explained earlier," he said sharply. "Smoking isn't allowed anywhere in this building. The sensors in the fire alarm are very sensitive."

He took the cigarette off her and carried it to the bathroom. She heard running water as he stubbed it out under the tap before returning.

"I'm sorry. It won't happen again. I am trying to give up, you know."

His eyes darted around the room. Had he guessed she was up to something?

"Very well. Mistakes do happen. I'll wish you goodnight. Again."

"Goodnight. I do hope I didn't wake up Allegra."

"Indeed." His tone was flat and gave nothing away.

Jessica sprang forward as the door shut. The foam had set and stopped the door from closing completely.

The lock clicked repeatedly. Fingers crossed Lyndon hadn't noticed anything was wrong and that she hadn't activated another alarm somewhere else in the building. She waited for a few minutes before daring to go out again, armed with her perfume bottle, powder compact and the mini torch disguised as a lipstick. She might as well give them all a try. Hopefully, she'd remember how to use them.

As she ran along the corridor to the emergency exit, she noticed the two cameras were completely obscured by foam. She darted through the door and flicked on her lipstick torch. The building was creepy at night. This was risky. Security guards would probably be roaming about but she couldn't waste this chance to see if anything sinister was going on. She padded down the stairs, looking for a way out. She ran down at least a hundred stairs, but she still couldn't find a single door. It was strange but maybe people in the main building had another emergency staircase. When she reached the bottom, she clutched her side, panting. Going up would be even worse. She urged herself through the only door she'd come across. This had to be the ground floor.

Now she had to be even more careful. It was impossible to get her bearings in the dark so she followed the corridor for a few minutes, keeping close to the walls. For some reason, she couldn't see any cameras on this floor. Suddenly, she heard voices. They came from the end of the corridor.

Security guards.

Jessica turned around and ran. Nightmare! She hadn't discovered anything useful yet. She stopped. The door was supposed to be here. She'd turned left, right and left again. Or was it right and then left? She looked over her shoulder. She could hear footsteps now. Had someone worked out she'd disabled the alarm and was out of her room? She ran further down the corridor, trying the pass on one door after another, but it was still inactive. She kept going until she found herself in a dead end.

Damnit.

She ran back up the corridor but it was too late. The voices were almost upon her. She remembered the emerald ring: she could laser a door open. She swiped the security pass against the sensor as she wriggled the ring off her finger. The door clicked and opened. The pass had finally worked. She didn't need a gadget. She pushed the ring back on and darted inside. She pulled the door almost shut, leaving it open a crack. A flash of torchlight illuminated two giant shadows on the walls.

"Are you sure you left it down here?" a man said.

"I can't remember," another answered.

He sounded nervous. The first man was probably more senior, she figured.

"We're wasting time. We've still got the west wing to check."

Two pairs of legs walked briskly past. She caught her breath. The guards had machine guns. Allegra obviously had to protect Teenosity before its launch to prevent rival firms getting hold of it and trying to imitate the formula, but were machine guns necessary? She had the horrible feeling these guards might panic and open fire if she startled them. She had to find a better hiding place. Carefully, she pulled the door shut. She crawled backwards and looked around. She was in the lab. That was why the pass had worked. The microscopes shone eerily in the darkness. She could make out the outlines of the fume cupboards and crawled towards them. She tried to tug one open but it was locked.

The security guards' voices were getting louder again. They were coming back. She looked around frantically. The clean room was a possibility. Ducking down, she ran across the lab. The door was locked but it was no good anyway. She'd be a sitting target. If the guards turned on the lights, they'd see her through the window. There weren't any hiding places.

"Maybe I left it in here." A voice boomed at the door.

They'd found her.

She had one last chance – the storeroom that Lyndon hadn't wanted her to see inside. She darted towards it and turned the door handle. It moved in her hand and she slipped in as the light flickered on. Footsteps pounded into the lab. She held her breath as she pressed her ear against the door.

"What's this?"

"Looks like lipstick."

She felt in her pocket. Her lipstick torch must have slipped out as she'd crawled across the floor. Luckily, she'd switched if off so they couldn't see its hidden function.

"We should probably raise the alarm," the man said.

"Do you think? This is a beauty company, for God's sake. There's bound to be lipsticks everywhere. A lab assistant probably dropped it."

"I'm sure it wasn't here earlier."

"Can't say I noticed. Look, what's the point of raising the alarm? It doesn't look like anything's missing. We're off in ten minutes. If we report it, we'll be here for another three hours. We'll have to search the whole building from top to bottom because of a stupid lipstick."

"But if we don't. . ." The man's voice trailed off.

She groaned inwardly. Even if they didn't find her straight away, Lyndon would discover she was missing from her room when the alarm sounded. She couldn't get back up to her floor in time without being spotted by patrols of security guards if a huge search was launched.

"Fine. I won't tell if you don't," the first man said. "Let's go."

The pair left the room, leaving her in darkness again. She waited a few minutes in case it was a trap and they were coming back for her. She looked around. Even though it was dark, she realized it wasn't a store cupboard. It was a good job she hadn't moved backwards. She was crouching at the top of a set of steep stairs.

CHAPTER
EIGHTEEN

Carefully, Jessica eased herself down the stairs on her bottom. She counted twenty-five steps before her foot struck something hard in front of her. It was a door.

"Let's see what clearance you have now, Mr Tarasaki," she said under her breath.

Jessica swiped the sensor and the door clicked open. This was definitely a part of AKSC that was off limits to visitors. She stepped into a large room that was dimly lit and piled high with cardboard boxes. It was a storage area with two doors. She guessed they probably led into loading bays. There was only one way to find out. She flicked open the lid of the silver compact and pressed the blue stone, aiming the X-ray vision at the first door. It was pretty simple to use even for a beginner like her. The compact revealed a corridor, heading deep into the bowels of the building.

She heard a muffled noise behind the second door. It sounded like the clanking of machinery, or was it a lorry reversing? Using the compact, she could see straight into a loading bay. Three – no, four – forklift trucks were loading boxes on to lorries. A dozen or so figures stood on the sidelines, standing guard. She recognized the outlines of their machine guns.

The armed guards were far enough away for her to slip through the door without attracting their attention. They were obviously watching the loading operation. To the left of the door lay a pile of boxes, which she could hide behind. She swiped the lock but the door didn't open. Mr Tarasaki had outlived his usefulness. It was time for more gadgets. She wriggled the emerald ring off her finger again, pointed it at the keypad and flicked the gem, making it spring open. She hesitated. Using a laser wasn't a good idea. She couldn't risk someone spotting a damaged lock.

Jessica slid the ring back on and scooped the blue stone out of the compact instead. She placed it next to the lock. Was that the right position? She had no idea.

Nathan hadn't gone into detail. She tried the lock. Nothing happened. She examined the stone. There had to be a way to turn it on. She fiddled with it and felt the base shift and click. Now what? Nathan hadn't said how long the electromagnetic pulse took to work either. Thirty seconds sounded good. She counted down and removed the stone, then tried the door. Hooray! It sprung open.

She crouched down and darted out, ducking behind the boxes. After a couple of seconds she peered out. Nobody had noticed. She watched the loading operation, which was being mounted with military precision. All the boxes were marked with "Teenosity" and "Paris" on the sides. Allegra was starting the distribution of her face cream across the French capital city.

Suddenly, a box fell off a forklift truck with a loud crash. The bottles spilled out and smashed, splashing the man closest to the lorry. He looked down at his trousers and brushed off the cream with his sleeve. He was trying to scoop up the mess when an alarm sounded and the guards sprang into action. One strode up to the bewildered man and marched him away from the spillage while another guard barked orders into a walkie-talkie. Five more men, all carrying equipment, arrived. They sprayed foam on to the damaged cardboard boxes and the smashed bottles of Teenosity.

One of the guards turned around, fixing a hard stare in her direction. She dodged back behind the boxes, her heart hammering wildly. Had he seen her? She couldn't hear anyone running towards her. She peered out again. Phew. He was concentrating on overseeing the clean-up operation again. Seconds later, Lyndon appeared, swiftly followed by Allegra. They marched up to him and all three became locked in a heated argument. Allegra's arms flailed about and she looked like she was going to punch the guard.

Lyndon intervened and pushed the man to one side. He put his arm around Allegra and pulled her close, kissing her protectively on her forehead. Theirs was clearly more than an employer/employee relationship. She steadied herself against the boxes. What on earth was going on? The guards had massively freaked out about the spillage. They'd completely overreacted.

Lyndon and Allegra were still arguing with the

guard as Jessica broke cover and ran to the door, which she'd wedged open with her real lipgloss. She used her compact X-ray vision at every corner as she retraced her steps back up to the lab and into the corridor as the alarm continued to sound. This time, she remembered where to find the door to the stairs. She took the steps two at a time, pausing halfway up to catch her breath.

Jessica didn't see any guards. Their attention was clearly focused on the spillage downstairs. The alarm finally stopped as she reached her floor. She used the compact one last time: the corridor was empty. She hesitated. Allegra and Lyndon were downstairs. She probably had a few minutes before Lyndon checked up on her. This could be her only opportunity to snoop around Allegra's suite. She ran down the corridor and stopped at a white door. The letters "A.K." were emblazoned in gold.

She tried the handle. The door opened and she slipped inside. The suite was like a larger version of hers: white, white and yet more white. One whole room was devoted to Allegra's clothes. She had rails upon rails of Diane von Furstenberg, Armani, Saint Laurent, Chanel, Christian Dior and Versace dresses, blouses, skirts, trousers and evening gowns. Jessica flicked through the hangers. Allegra had labelled all the clothes with the date she'd worn them. She couldn't have worn anything twice. She'd also fitted the room with wall-to-wall mirrors, allowing her to see herself from every angle as she dressed. The next room was full of designer shoes, including Manolo Blahniks, Louboutins and Jimmy Choos. Allegra easily had three hundred pairs.

Jessica padded to the study and tried the drawers of the desk. They didn't contain anything remotely interesting, just expensive-looking AKSC headed notepaper and other stationery. She doubled back and went into the en-suite bathroom. Surprise, surprise, it was all white. What did she have against colour?

She peeped in the bathroom cabinets. They were lined with AKSC anti-ageing eye, neck, face and body creams. She went back into the bedroom and pulled open the drawer of the bedside table. Inside was a neat row of large white files. She pulled one out. It was all about Allegra. She'd kept a detailed record of her career dating back to when she was a successful child model, working for different clothing lines. By the age of fourteen, she'd won a major modelling competition, according to a newspaper article. Jessica's eyes rested on another cutting on the opposite page, from the *London Evening Standard* in August 1961.

London socialite Valerie Knight, 38, died in a freak accident at her West Kensington home yesterday.

Mrs Knight suffered a broken neck after falling down the stairs at the home she shared with billionaire businessman Wesley Knight and her 14-year-old stepdaughter, Allegra Knight.

The former waitress was renowned for her parties, which were attended by London's wealthiest and most connected people, and was a regular fixture on magazine best-dressed lists.

Mr Knight's first wife, Rosemary, died of cancer ten years ago.

She'd obviously had a really tough childhood – losing her mum aged four like she had, and then her stepmother. It totally sucked, and might explain some of her strange behaviour. Who wouldn't be traumatized by that? Jessica flicked over. Page after page detailed Allegra's rise to the top of the modelling world. She'd kept press clippings about her retirement and the launch of AKSC.

Jessica picked up another file. It was full of cuttings about Tyler, dating back years. Allegra had been following her career ever since she was scouted by Lydia Hollings at Athens International Airport. She'd collected photographs from her catwalk shows and advertising campaigns for Naturissmo SkinCare as well as newspaper cuttings and magazine articles. She'd underlined facts she'd found interesting, such as *Vogue* announcing Tyler had unexpectedly dropped out of her first solo cover shoot. Jessica fished out a third file. This one was all about Jacey's career. She checked the others. Allegra had dedicated a file to each of the famous five.

She paused as she came to the last page of Olinka's file. It was another photo from Emerald's fiftieth anniversary ball. Allegra stood next to the famous five, but this time she'd scribbled over their faces in black biro with such force it had left holes in the picture. Jessica slammed the file shut and picked up the last one from the drawer. She guessed before opening it what she'd find inside.

Fingers trembling, she checked. She was right. The file was all about *her*. Allegra had cut out an article about her signing to Primus, along with her teen covers. She flicked over the page and found the photo from her *Teen Mode* shoot. Her eyes had been completely scratched out with the same black biro.

The file slipped through her fingers.

Allegra hated them all. That was clear. Could she have been responsible for the famous five vanishing? Margurita had mentioned the plastic surgery rumour. Had Allegra recommended a dodgy plastic surgeon on purpose at the ball out of spite? It seemed far-fetched, but it was the last time the girls had been seen in public. Why did everyone who came into contact with Allegra disappear – Sam, the famous five, her dad? She shivered. What happened to them? Could she be next?

She shoved the files back into the drawer as the suite door clicked open. Allegra was back. Jessica didn't want to be trapped in the bedroom or en-suite bathroom so she ran into the dressing room, squeezing in-between a rail of evening gowns. She heard Allegra walk into the room, humming softly, as she undressed. Then silence. Jessica froze. Had Allegra spotted her? She hadn't heard her walk past into her bedroom. Was she still in the room? Cautiously, Jessica peered out.

Allegra stood completely naked in front of the mirrors, her clothes in a heap by her feet. She smoothed her forehead and pinched an imaginary roll of fat on her waist and beneath her arms. She checked her bottom in the mirror and tweaked her thighs, leaving vivid red marks, as she sobbed loudly. She fled into the bedroom and slammed the door. Jessica slid out of her hiding place. She'd seen enough. Allegra was a total basket case.

She flicked open her compact behind the door, making sure the corridor was empty. She'd almost made it to her room when she heard a *ping*. She spun around and pretended to be walking towards the lift.

"Jessica?" Lyndon stepped out, frowning. "What are you doing out here?"

"I heard the alarm go off earlier. I thought there must be a fire. I wanted to find out what was going on."

"So you got dressed and brought your face

powder?" He stared at the compact in her hand.

What would Sara do now? She flicked the compact open and pulled out her lipgloss, applying a slick.

"Well, you know models. We're a vain bunch. We like to look good at all times." She snapped the compact shut with a bright smile.

"I see," Lyndon said. "Well, there's no need to be worried. You can return to your room now."

"OK, but why *did* the alarm go off?"

"We had a minor incident in the loading bay, that's all."

"Really? What happened?"

Anger flashed across his face. "Nothing that concerns you." Stroking his beard, he softened. "What I meant to say is you shouldn't be unduly concerned. A worker accidentally dropped a box on his foot as he loaded the lorries with Teenosity."

"Ouch! That had to hurt."

"It's nothing more serious than a fractured toe, but we take security – and safety – seriously here. The alarm system is activated as part of normal protocol."

"Is he OK? The worker, I mean?"

"He's fine. He's being checked out at hospital. Now if you'll excuse me, I must report back to Miss Knight. Goodnight."

"Goodnight." She closed the door, her heart beating rapidly.

Lyndon had lied. The worker hadn't hurt his foot. In fact, he hadn't been injured at all. What was going on?

She wondered if he'd guessed she'd been exploring. More importantly, would Allegra notice her files had been tampered with? If so, Jessica was in serious trouble.

She jammed a chair under the door handle for extra peace of mind and whipped out Becky's phone. She'd bypass MI6 and ring the police direct. Her French was good enough to get a number for the local station from the operator. It couldn't be legal to have security guards armed with machine guns on private premises. They weren't wearing uniforms so they couldn't be gendarmes. The police would have to get a search warrant. Nathan wouldn't be able to stop them. She'd be able to direct them to the corridors in the basement, which were definitely worth a further look. Dad could be down there.

Blast.

Becky's phone was completely dead. She tried her own mobile but that was dead too. How was that even remotely possible? She'd charged both phones that morning and there'd been enough juice to text Mattie before she left the room. She tried taking the batteries out and putting them in again but they still didn't work. She picked up the landline phone, which gave a few rings.

"Hello. Housekeeping?"

She put the receiver down. She couldn't get an outside line, but there was another way. She grabbed her make-up bag and emptied it on to the bed, then grabbed the eyeshadow palette and flicked open the lid. The compact contained six small palettes of light blue and silver eyeshadow. Using a hairgrip, she unclipped the middle palette as Nathan had instructed and pressed a tiny button in the space. The gadget bleeped as it stirred to life. The lid lit up, forming a tiny computer screen with a keyboard illuminated beneath it.

Using the hairgrip again, she opened a new memo

and immediately hit a snag. Nathan said a central MI6 email address would pop up automatically on any email. It didn't. Crucially, he hadn't explained what to do if it didn't work. Her hunch was right. This was the most important gadget that gave her contact with the outside world and it was useless. Either it had malfunctioned or, more likely, Nathan had deliberately sabotaged it so she couldn't alert MI6. If the address wasn't something she could guess, like helpme@MI6.co.uk, she was seriously screwed. She had to think of something else.

She didn't have an email address for Margaret. Mattie didn't use computers and MI6 had confiscated their home ones anyway. The only email address she could remember off by heart was Becky's. She was her lifeline right now. For the next hour, she painstakingly typed out what she'd seen at the loading bay and in Allegra's suite. She described how she believed Nathan was behind an attempt on her life and that she suspected he was Starfish, a treacherous double agent. She added in Mattie's telephone number.

Call MI6 headquarters in London and ask for Nathan and Margaret's boss, Mrs T. Tell her to raid the building, she typed carefully. *If she stonewalls you, telephone the Met police. You're my only hope, Becky. I know you won't let me down. BFF.*

She pressed send and watched the message disappear. Becky was bound to be online. She was always browsing agents' websites and reading up about RADA and famous actresses. Hopefully, she'd check her emails soon. Now all Jessica could do was wait.

CHAPTER
NINETEEN

A chauffeur-driven limo arrived at six thirty a.m. and took Jessica to a large derelict chemical factory on the edge of Paris. The driver kept the doors locked and the partition screen up during the journey so she couldn't ask to borrow his mobile or charger. From a distance, the large steel columns rose majestically into the air, but as the car finally glided through the barbed-wire-covered gates, an air of decay crept over the site. The rusting steel tanks had been long abandoned and weeds sprouted up through the latticework of pipes. A sulphurous smell greeted Jessica's nostrils as she climbed out of the car. It looked like somewhere a mobster would carry out a hit, not a location for a modelling shoot.

The sight of an ambulance parked outside the building didn't steady her nerves. A paramedic eyed her curiously as he puffed on a cigarette. He nodded towards a door. She picked her way over rusty girders and potholed, cracked concrete, through the heavy, wrought-iron door. It banged shut behind her, scaring a couple of pigeons.

She dug her fingers into the palms of her hands to calm her nerves. She hesitated at the foot of a set of dilapidated stairs. Paint had peeled off the walls and something smelt rotten. This didn't feel right at all.

"Up here!" a voice boomed.

She grabbed the rusty iron stair rail and looked up. It rattled precariously beneath her fingers, making her nerves even more ragged. The one thing she hated more than snakes was heights. This building looked *high*. Her acrophobia had never been an issue in modelling until now. Her heart beat louder and louder as she climbed higher and higher and there was a ringing noise in her ears. She kept her eyes fixed firmly on the step in front of her as she picked her way over a desiccated rat, lying outstretched on its back. The whole building had a smell of death about it. Within a few minutes she'd reached the top. A gust of wind brushed her face. She took a deep breath to steady herself and looked down at her hands. They were dyed red from the rails. It looked like they were covered in blood.

"Welcome, Jessica!"

A thin, pale-faced man wearing a plain white shirt and chinos lunged forward and shook her hand vigorously. She recognized him instantly and almost flung herself into his arms. She wasn't there to be murdered. It was Ferdinand Lathos. He'd shot covers for every glossy in the world, including American, French, British and Italian *Vogue*, and had done advertising campaigns for the likes of Burberry and Louis Vuitton.

"I hope you're not afraid of heights because this shoot is my most adventurous yet." He smiled encouragingly at her.

She gulped and shook her head. How could she admit her stomach lurched dangerously at the thought of standing sixty feet up on the sixth floor of the building? She closed her eyes as her stomach did another somersault. She felt Ferdinand link his arm in hers, pulling her forward.

"Today, I'm going to suspend you from a crane and you'll fly for me," he said.

She looked down at her feet. Now she stood on the edge of a large hole. She could see right down to the concrete at the bottom. The ground surged up to meet her, throwing her off balance. She couldn't focus on anything. It was all blurred. Her throat tightened.

"No flying yet." He laughed, mistaking her near fainting for unbridled enthusiasm. "You have to be fitted with a safety harness and wires first before you fly like a bird for me."

The only thing she could feel soar was breakfast, threatening to propel itself out of her stomach. She couldn't do this, she really couldn't. Before she could protest, she was steered away to a large group of make-up artists and stylists. Ferdinand jabbered on about how the shoot would be the epitome of "urban chic". He wanted strong make-up and smoky eyes to contrast with her floaty silver chiffon Marc Jacobs evening gown.

"I'm looking for an urban warrior, strong yet graceful," he said before darting away to set up his cameras and lights.

Her hands were sweaty and she wanted to throw up. Repeatedly. There wouldn't be anything graceful about heaving her guts up in front of everyone. She closed her eyes as her hair was lacquered and put into large rollers. Her nails were painted black while her face was made up. A man attached long silver false eyelashes and sprayed her cheeks with silver paint. A stylist helped her into a specially adapted harness, followed by a long silver dress with a sprinkling of sequins at the hem. He explained it had been altered to allow safety wires to poke through. After a make-up artist performed the finishing touches, she was finally ready.

"What about her bangle?" a stylist asked, pointing to the silver bracelet clamped on her wrist.

"I like it. It's modern. It's very much the look I'm after. Strong, and solid," Ferdinand said. "But let's lose the necklace. It's *so* yesteryear."

She wanted to tell him her mum's pendant was the most precious thing she owned, but she knew he wouldn't care. She removed the necklace and handed it to an assistant for safekeeping. Had Becky checked her emails yet and rung MI6? She might not have to go through with this if AKSC had been raided already.

"Can I borrow your phone?" she said, turning to a stylist. "Mine's not working."

The woman shook her head. "It's a mobile-free shoot. Nobody's allowed to bring them. Apparently Ferdinand finds mobiles too distracting when he's working. He goes mad if he even hears a text message beep."

Jessica bit her lip as two stylists steered her towards the hole. So this was what it felt like to be marched to your death. Luc, a stunt coordinator, explained how the harness would work. The factory was already fitted with a lifting beam and winch on each floor, which had moved process tanks and pumps when the building was full of chemical equipment instead of make-up artists and stylists. He'd managed to rig a winch to raise her off the ground, using safety wires attached to the lifting beam. The wires were clipped into her harness through the dress. Two wires were positioned at her side and the third from her back.

"There's no possibility of falling," he said.

"Then why is an ambulance here?"

"That's for insurance reasons. It's a legal requirement in the event of the impossible."

She shivered as he fastened the wires into place. The impossible scared her the most. Ferdinand bounded over. He was so excited by the shoot she didn't dare tell him she couldn't go through with it. He explained he'd be shooting from the floor below, so she would appear to be diving down towards him. His assistant was taking photographs from this floor. She nodded, unable to speak. Her mouth was horribly dry.

Before she could ask for water, she was winched off the ground and steered towards the edge, almost in a horizontal position. She closed her eyes as a blast of wind rustled her dress. She had to stay calm. She wasn't in any danger. She could do this if she didn't look down.

"Fantastic. Now begin!" Ferdinand bellowed instructions from the floor below. "I need strong, forceful looks. A girl who uses Teenosity can soar to greatness."

She willed her eyes to open and immediately

swung into "work mode", striking her first pose. The movement was too sudden and it threw her off balance, sending her twirling like a puppet on a string.

Help, help, help, the voice inside her head screamed.

"Balance yourself," Ferdinand shouted. "You need to get used to the sensation. Try again."

She obeyed. This time it was easier. She managed to move her body slowly and strongly so as not to unbalance the wires.

"Fabulous, Jessica! I love your determined look. Now give me vulnerable."

That wouldn't be hard. How vulnerable would he feel if all that stopped him from plunging sixty feet to his death were a couple of wires? The thought actually brought a smile to her face.

"Excellent!" Ferdinand cried. "I love it. Give me more!"

The shoot was exhausting, as Ferdinand insisted on working through while he still had good light. Finally, he agreed to stop for a short break at three p.m., and Jessica wolfed down a brie and tomato baguette. She was ravenous with nerves. After she ate, the make-up artists patiently reapplied her "face" and the stylists rearranged her hair and dress. It was time to be strapped into place again. She felt less nervous, as she'd already done it once. How much worse could it be? Maybe she was finally beginning to conquer her fears. As she approached the hole, she noticed a tall, stocky assistant, clad in jeans and a black bomber jacket, lingering next to the winch system. His back was turned.

"Get away from there," Luc said indignantly. "I'm the only one who's authorized to operate the crane."

The man moved away, stumbling over a cable. She watched him retreat, pulling his blue baseball cap down low. She couldn't see his face properly but she was sure he hadn't been on set earlier.

As the crane winched her over the hole, she lifted her arms to give the impression she was flying. Suddenly, a loud grinding noise above her head sent a chilling ripple through her body. Luc let out a loud shout and she heard a deathly crack. The harness jolted, sending the wires spinning. She plunged through the hole head first.

"No!" she screamed.

She caught a flash of Ferdinand's horrified face

as she fell through his floor to the next, the wire unwinding like a ball of string. Shouts rang out above her head. The force of the wind kept her eyes firmly pinned open and she could see the ground hurtling towards her. She was going to die. The thought was like a shot of adrenaline. She had to stop herself.

How?

Think, think, think. She was almost at the bottom.

The Spider-Woman bracelet! She clawed at it desperately. She found the tiny clasp, pulled the knob and aimed at a steel girder. She could hear whirring before being violently yanked upwards. The impact was brutal. There was a loud crack and a burning pain shot up her arm as her shoulder was wrenched out of joint. The safety equipment fell around her, leaving her dangling helplessly by the wrist. She looked down. The ground was a metre away. With a racking sob, she released the bracelet catch and crashed on to concrete. As she looked up, the man in the baseball cap ran out of the warehouse.

Blackness enveloped her like a warm, suffocating blanket.

*

It took her a while to realize where she was. She definitely wasn't lying in a hospital bed. She touched the white quilt. It was expensive – made from the finest silk. Her white bathrobe was luxuriously soft and smelt of roses. She looked at the photos on the walls and a small white sofa with scatter cushions. White again. She groaned. She was back in Allegra's guest suite. She looked across and saw her mum's necklace on the bedside table. Next to it was a clock. It was eight p.m. She'd been unconscious for hours.

She eased herself up slowly, wincing at the dull, throbbing pain in her shoulder. She tugged her sweater and jeans off a chair and gingerly pulled them on. She'd dislocated her shoulder in the fall but someone had put it back into place. They must have given her some drugs to take the edge off the pain. She felt woozy but she could still remember what had happened. The winch system had failed. It was unlikely to have been an accident. The man with the baseball cap must have tampered with it. He'd tried to kill her. If it hadn't been for the Spider-Woman bracelet, he'd have succeeded. Nathan would kick himself for giving it to her. He probably hadn't thought that would work either.

She dangled a foot out of bed and pulled her bag towards her. Someone had brought it back. She checked her phones. They were still dead. She pulled out the eyeshadow palette from her make-up bag and was about to flick it open and send another email when the door opened. Allegra appeared, sporting enormous dark sunglasses and a cream trouser suit. A Burberry scarf was knotted tightly around her neck.

"Going somewhere?" She glided towards her.

"I'm leaving." Jessica stood up. "I'm hardly going to stay when someone's tried to kill me on your shoot."

"I'm afraid I can't let you do that." Allegra stood in front of her, hands clamped firmly on her slender hips.

"You can't stop me." Jessica grabbed her bag and pushed past her to the door. Allegra was a size zero and looked as fragile as one of Sam's paper swans. Jessica could easily kick-box her way out of the room if she needed to.

Allegra caught her hand, a smile hovering on her frozen lips.

Jessica felt a sharp, stabbing pain in her arm and her legs collapsed beneath her. She slumped on to the carpet and looked down at her arm. A syringe stuck out of it.

Allegra bent down. "It's fast-acting poison," she whispered in Jessica's ear. "You'll be paralysed for hours – enough time for us to launch Teenosity."

Jessica tried to speak but her lips were numb. She couldn't move her legs either. They were too heavy. She couldn't get up. She stared helplessly at the ceiling. The lights were sharp diamonds, piercing her eyeballs.

"There's no point fighting it." Allegra laughed as the door opened.

Jessica couldn't turn her head. Her eyes swivelled to the left, her heart beating furiously. It was the man in the blue baseball cap again. He'd returned to finish her off.

"Is she out yet?" Lyndon removed the cap.

"Almost. Just a few seconds longer."

"We don't have time to waste, darling." He picked Jessica up and threw her down on the bed like a rag doll.

"If you'd done your job properly with the wire today or even with poisoning that blasted dress

245

yesterday, I wouldn't have to tie up loose endings now, *darling*," Allegra answered sweetly. "Starfish must think you're terribly incompetent when you can't follow his simple instructions."

"Touché," Lyndon said, "but I wasn't to know that daddy's little helper would come equipped with some kind of safety rope, was I? Starfish forgot to tell us that bit of useful info when he suggested cutting the wire. And it's hardly my fault that Jessica changed dresses at the last minute. Forging a backstage pass is one thing, but clairvoyance is another. Even Starfish doesn't have that talent."

"Of course, dear. Whatever you say." She snatched the eyeshadow palette out of Jessica's frozen hand. "I don't need to guess whose handiwork this is." Allegra scooped up her mum's necklace from the bedside table and dropped it into her jacket pocket.

"You should double-check with Starfish what other gadgets she's got," Lyndon murmured. "They could be useful to us." He rummaged in her make-up bag, examining lipsticks and an eyeshadow applicator.

Allegra stared down at Jessica. "You don't mind, do you, Jessica? You won't need MI6 goodies ever again.

I've already left word with Camille that you've decided to return to London. No one can help you."

She leant down until her lips were almost touching Jessica's ear. Her perfume was sickly and suffocating.

"Especially not your father," she added. "Jack's not feeling well today. I'm worried about him. Who knows how long a man in his condition will last without his medication? I'm guessing not long, given what he's been through."

Jessica tried to open her mouth but her whole body was frozen. A veil of blackness slowly fell behind her eyes, shutting everything else out. She couldn't fight it. The drugs were too strong. She watched Allegra leave the room. Lyndon followed, clutching her make-up bag. As she slipped away, one word remained imprinted in her mind like blood in fresh snow.

Dad.

CHAPTER
TWENTY

Jessica soared through the sky in a helicopter. In front of her was the pilot. Someone sat next to him. Her long blonde hair was tied into an untidy ponytail and her face was obscured.

"Mum!"

She turned around and smiled, her eyes crinkling at the corners. "Don't worry, jellybean. Everything's going to be OK, trust me."

The helicopter coughed and spluttered.

"What's wrong? What's happening?"

"I don't know." Her mum turned away again.

"No! Do something!"

Jessica shook the pilot but he flopped forward. She grabbed for the controls.

"It's too late," her mum said calmly. "There's nothing you can do. We have to accept our fate. There's no other way, Jessica. Nathan said we're expendable. He was right."

"Help me, Mum, please!"

The helicopter nosedived into a steep descent. The ground hurtled towards her. They were going to crash. She couldn't do anything to stop it.

"Mum!"

Her eyes flew open. Her breath was raw and ragged, hurting her ribs and throat with every gasp. She was alive. Just. Every bone in her body and every inch of her skin screamed with pain. Her head felt heavy and she couldn't think straight. It was like trying to see through thick pea-soup fog. She had to concentrate.

Think. What had happened?

There was a syringe. It was stuck in her arm. Allegra had stabbed her with it. She'd been drugged and partially paralysed. She tried to move and managed to wriggle her toes but the effort exhausted her. She rested for a couple of minutes until she had enough strength to push herself on to her side. The movement made her head swim. She was violently sick until she had nothing left to bring up.

Emptying her stomach made her feel better. The room had stopped spinning and her arms and legs tingled as the feeling flooded back. She looked at the clock on the bedside table. It was six thirty a.m., the day of Teenosity's launch. She'd been knocked out all night. She swung her legs out of bed and stood up. Her legs crumpled beneath her and she fell to the carpet.

Get up, get up, get up. She breathed through her mouth, trying to control the waves of nausea. She wasn't going to lie here, waiting for Allegra to come back and kill her. She grabbed the side of the bed. Carefully, she pulled herself into a sitting-up position and closed her eyes. As soon as the dizziness passed, she used the bed to lever herself up. Slowly, she got to her feet.

The room lurched and she collapsed on to the bed. She waited a couple of minutes, until she felt steady enough to try again. Focusing on the door, she stood up and managed three steps before stumbling. Again, she picked herself up and staggered on. It was only a small distance but it felt like miles. This time, she caught the handle as she fell and the door swung open. The alarm had been disabled. She heaved herself up. Now, she was in the hallway aiming for the lift. The muscles in her legs grew stronger with every step.

Jessica hammered on the lift button, praying Allegra or Lyndon wouldn't reappear. She was far too weak to fight them off. The lift opened and she hauled herself inside, sinking to her heels as it glided down to the ground floor. The doors opened. A dark, empty corridor led to reception. Was it a trap? Was someone waiting for her by the doors? It had to be a possibility. She could reach safety in a matter of seconds. Once outside, she could alert the police.

She hesitated as she stepped out. What had Allegra whispered in her ear? Her dad was sick. She couldn't leave him here. She had to find Sam too. They must be somewhere in the building. They were the loose ends Allegra had to be planning to tie up. She turned her back on her escape route and staggered away. She had to get to the basement.

Jessica managed to get to the lab by steadying herself against the walls. She pulled herself through the door at the back of the lab and slowly went down the stairs on her bottom, stopping and resting every couple of minutes. She stood up and pushed the door. It had already been deactivated and just swung open.

She staggered through the room and peered around the door leading to the loading bay. All the lorries and boxes had gone. The drivers must have already distributed Teenosity across Paris. She ducked back inside and opened the next door, revealing a narrow corridor. A single door was on her right. It could be another storage room.

Something banged. It sounded like a door slamming shut close by. Now she could hear voices. They were getting louder. She looked about. She couldn't escape or put up much of a fight. She had to get inside the room. She tried the door but this one didn't automatically open. She dug out the security pass she'd used the previous night. Luckily, Allegra hadn't bothered to search the back pockets of her jeans. She'd never told Nathan about the pass either, so Allegra hadn't known to look for it.

Please let it work.

She swiped the bar and the door slid open, revealing

darkness. She threw herself inside as two security guards rounded the corner. She pressed her ear to the door as they stomped past. They hadn't heard her. She looked about. A weak light lit up the room. It was another lab, but this one was small and cramped. The fusty smell reminded her of chemistry lessons back at school. An old man was fast asleep on a camp bed in the corner, a blanket thrown across his thin, frail legs. He had a shock of white hair and his face was crinkled and tortoise-like.

His eyes flew open. They were as bright as fresh cornflowers, contrasting with his skin, which was coarse and heavily lined like old parchment paper. His eyes darted from her to the door as if he were trying to calculate something. He leapt agilely off the bed and dived into the corner, shrouding his face in darkness. She was taken aback. He'd moved quickly for someone so old.

"Who are you?" he said.

"My name's Jessica—" she began.

"Well, Jessica, you can go straight back to Allegra and tell her the answer's still no. I won't do it any more. She's done her worst and I won't change my mind. She can't get anything else out of me."

She blinked. If she hadn't seen his face, she could have sworn his voice belonged to a much younger man.

"Allegra doesn't know I'm here," she said. "I sneaked past security to try and find my dad. Have you seen him? His name's Jack Cole. He's missing."

The man looked away and didn't reply.

"Please help me," she said, edging closer.

He shrank back against the wall.

"I haven't seen him," he said, "but I've heard the name before."

"Did Allegra mention him? What did she say? Please try and remember."

"It doesn't matter now. It's too late."

"What do you mean?" Her heart rattled against her ribcage. She'd come this far; she couldn't be too late.

His blue eyes bored into her face. "Allegra said he was looking for me but he walked straight into a trap and now he's paying for snooping around. Apparently he's a very a sick man."

She steadied herself against the wall. "Is he still alive?" Her voice sounded thin and reedy, like that of a bird's. She almost couldn't bear to hear his answer.

"I think so," he said, "but probably not for much longer. Allegra can't risk him getting out of here and talking. She'll never let him go."

"Where is he?"

The man shrugged. "Somewhere here, I guess, unless they've moved him already."

"But why was he looking for *you*? It doesn't make any sense."

"I don't know," he replied, "but it's possible my mum hired him after I went missing. It's the sort of practical thing she'd do."

He emerged from the shadows and sat on the bed, his head in his hands.

"That can't be right," she said. "My dad came here to look for Sam Bishop. He's a thirty-four-year-old nanotechnologist who used to work here. Have you seen him?"

The man looked up and laughed softly. Tears rolled down his face.

"What's so funny?"

He wiped his eyes on the cuff of his grey, stained shirt. "You wouldn't believe me if I told you."

"Try me."

He stared deep into her eyes. "I'm Sam Bishop."

She tried to speak but no words came out.

The man burst out laughing again. "You see! I said you wouldn't believe me. No one will." His voice was manic and high-pitched.

"But that's impossible. You can't be Sam. I've seen the photo. He's—"

"A young man?"

She nodded.

"I am a young man but now I'm trapped inside the body of an old man."

She sat on the bed next to him. He was clearly insane. He couldn't have gone from the age of thirty-four to eighty in the space of over two months. It was a physical impossibility, wasn't it?

"Allegra told me even if I managed to escape, nobody would ever believe me," he said. "I'd be declared insane and locked up somewhere. I'm as good as dead already. If I do ever get out, I can't go home. How can I turn up on my mum's doorstep looking like this? She'd drop dead of a heart attack."

She stared at him, shocked. He was deadly serious. She remembered how Lyndon had talked about Sam using nanotechnology to make Teenosity.

"The nanorobots in Teenosity were supposed to halt the ageing process," she said slowly.

He gave a bitter laugh. "The experiments always went wrong in the final stages for some reason. It was a total disaster."

Jessica stared at his wrinkles. It was unthinkable. Yet it was the only logical explanation.

"Teenosity did the reverse," she gasped. "It speeded up ageing."

"Exactly. When I told Allegra the ageing process was being accelerated, she lost it. Big time. You see, she'd convinced herself there'd be a cure for ageing in her lifetime."

He sprang to his feet and paced the room.

"She made me work fourteen-hour days to try and find the correct formula. Eventually I'd had enough and told her I was quitting. She demanded my notes, and that's when I made the biggest mistake of my life. I was stupid."

He paused and fiddled with a row of test tubes on the counter.

"What did you do?" she said.

"I told her I didn't make notes. My work was in here." He turned around and tapped his lined forehead. "I managed to make it out of her suite and get into the lift without being stopped. I hadn't even bothered to go back to the lab to fetch my bag. I just wanted to get the hell out. I think I'd reached the third floor when Lyndon got in. He stuck a needle in my thigh and I blacked out. When I woke up, I was here."

"That's terrible. I'm so sorry." Jessica looked down and noticed she'd picked the skin around her nail again. It was bleeding. Had her dad been ambushed like that as he returned to his hotel that night? He'd almost made it back before he was snatched. He could have broken free inside AKSC days later and managed to make his Code Red call.

"That was just the start of it," Sam said. "Later that night, Allegra told me the plans had changed. I had to continue making the faulty nanorobots. I couldn't understand it. I told her I wouldn't, that I was going to the police and I'd have her arrested for assault and imprisonment. She laughed and said if I refused to cooperate, she'd have my mum killed. Everyone knew most of her guards were ex-cons. What else could I do?"

He shivered as he folded his arms across his thin body.

"You had no choice. It wasn't your fault."

"I guess not, but it didn't make it feel any better. I was trapped. A guard had emptied my hotel room. He brought everything to me here, along with some equipment to use during the day. At night, I was escorted back up to the main lab to work. It was the same routine, day in day out, for weeks. A few nights ago I managed to drop a paper swan in the hope someone would see it and realize it belonged to me. I was always making origami."

"I found it! That's how I knew Allegra was lying about your disappearance."

"So it did work." His face broke into a smile for the first time, making his teeth look unnaturally white and healthy against his skin. "I thought Allegra would come to her senses and realize my work was pointless, but if anything she became even more obsessed. I worked around the clock to produce the nanorobots single-handedly, as she didn't trust anyone else to help me. Three weeks into my captivity, I tried to escape, but I must have triggered an alarm. Her guards stormed in and I was knocked out and drugged again."

"And Allegra did this to you?" She shuddered.

"When I woke up, Allegra said it was time to do a proper test. Up until then, I'd been experimenting on single skin cells and nothing more. Allegra said she couldn't bear animal testing."

He sat back down on the bed and wept.

"You don't have to talk about it if you don't want to," she said, resting a hand on his shoulder.

He shook it off. "No, I need to. I want people to know what she did to me."

He took a deep breath before continuing.

"The guards tied me to the bed and Allegra arrived with a test tube of my formula. I begged her not to do it. I explained the damage to a human body would be extreme and irreversible. She laughed and said she hoped it would be. I struggled but there was nothing I could do."

He closed his eyes and gripped the side of the bed.

"A guard clamped his hand over my nose and forced my head back. Allegra poured the liquid in. I didn't feel anything at first except panic, but soon the pain was excruciating. It was as if the skin was being peeled off every muscle in my body. I passed out. When I finally woke up, the deterioration had stabilized and I looked like this."

"I don't know what to say. It's so awful." She tried to focus on the glass bottles on the counter as blood rushed to her head. Had her dad suffered the same fate? There was no way he could survive it with M.S.

"In a way I'm lucky," Sam continued. "I could easily have died. I'm fit and young so my body was able to withstand the accelerated ageing process without packing up completely. It could have killed someone weaker. Not that Allegra cared. She said I was a successful dummy run. She had five other test subjects lined up. Who they are, I have no idea."

"Ohmigod. The famous five."

Tyler. Olinka. Jacey. Darice. Valeriya.

They drank champagne at Emerald's fiftieth anniversary ball while Allegra stuck to orange juice. She'd kept their photo on the wall as a trophy. A reminder of her crime. She'd poisoned them with

Teenosity.

"Forgive me for asking, but who are the famous five?"

"Five supermodels. Allegra met them at a ball in London before Christmas and they all quit modelling shortly afterwards. No one's seen them in public since. They're rumoured to have had plastic surgery."

"They'd need it after this." Sam shook his head slowly. "But why would Allegra want to hurt *them*?"

Jessica remembered Allegra's accusation, the first time they'd met, about her wanting to steal her crown. She seemed to resent giving her a big modelling break.

"Perhaps she was jealous of their success. She got through the VIP cordon at the ball and must have spiked their champagne somehow."

"It's certainly possible if she contaminated the whole bottle and poured out five glasses herself," Sam said. "The liquid's tasteless and odourless, so the models wouldn't have noticed anything was wrong at first."

"But why weren't they rushed to hospital straight away if this is what happened to them?" She gestured to Sam's wizened face. "It'd have been headline news.

Instead, they just vanished."

He frowned, running a liver-spotted hand through his white hair.

"Allegra must have amended the dosage," he explained. "She'd have known the amount she gave me was far too drastic for those girls. She'd have been arrested on the spot if they'd collapsed at the ball. People would have known she'd spiked their drinks. But she could have put a tiny drop into the champagne bottle. The deterioration of skin cells would have been a lot slower. It could have taken days to act and the ageing wouldn't have been as dramatic, particularly if the girls only had a few sips."

"But it was still enough to ruin their careers and their lives." It was Jessica's turn to pace the lab. "Allegra knew Emerald would try and hush the whole thing up instead of drawing attention to their disfigurements. The agency sent them away for plastic surgery in Switzerland before anyone realized what was wrong."

"That's why Allegra has to be stopped before she does this to anyone else," Sam said urgently. "If she catches you here, you could be her next victim. Failing to launch Teenosity has tipped her completely over the edge."

"But Teenosity *is* going on sale, from this morning. I saw boxes being loaded on to lorries last night. Allegra's already distributed Teenosity across Europe in time for the launch today."

"What?" He jumped to his feet. "That can't be allowed to happen. Allegra can't possibly realize the implications—"

"Oh, I realize the implications, Sam. You're the naïve fool who still hasn't realized what I'm capable of."

Allegra stood in the doorway, flanked by guards on either side. Her powdered face was masklike and for once she wasn't wearing sunglasses. Her blue eyes glittered dangerously.

CHAPTER
TWENTY ONE

"I'm insulted you don't think I know what I'm doing," Allegra said. "I've dreamt about my revenge night after night. I've plotted it for weeks, months, years."

"Revenge for what, exactly?" Jessica demanded. "What has anyone ever done to you?"

Allegra let out a brittle laugh. "Do you have any idea what it was like to be discarded by Emerald all those years ago? I was devastated. I felt so worthless and depressed I couldn't get out of bed for months."

She closed her eyes as she tucked her hair behind her ears, revealing huge diamond studs.

"Now all those stupid young girls will get to know what it feels like to be treated like a piece of trash. Why should I age alone when I can have company?

Why should I be tortured by staring at gorgeous young faces on the cover of magazines? My magazines? It's too much to bear."

"You're crazy," Jessica said. "You can't possibly think you'll get away with this."

"But I already have, darling." Allegra cackled loudly. "Your father couldn't stop me and neither can you. You both walked into a trap. Did you *really* think I'd want to employ the girl next door to represent my company? Once you arrived in Paris, it quickly became apparent you'd find a way to snoop around here. It made much more sense to invite you in and get rid of you as well. Two for the price of one. It was just a shame we had to ruin an Alexander McQueen gown in the process."

Jessica bit her lip. Her instincts *were* right. Nathan had tried to keep her away from AKSC at first but then the plan changed and he sent her into a trap without any backup and the dodgy eyeshadow palette – a crucial gadget that he knew wouldn't work.

"In a few weeks' time, when those silly little girls realize there's something wrong with the cream, it'll be too late," Allegra continued. "There'll be nothing they can do to reverse the ageing process. They'll be stuck with their ugly faces for the rest of their lives like Tyler and the others."

"But you'll be caught and thrown into prison," Jessica said. "How is that revenge when you get to spend the rest of your life locked up? You'll have thrown away everything you've ever worked for."

"Wrong again. Starfish has arranged my new passport, safe passage out of the country and a new identity in exchange for a single vial of the Teenosity formula. It is, after all, unique and extremely valuable."

She whipped a small metal canister out of her handbag and waved it at Jessica.

"For God's sake, put it down," Sam shouted. "If the lid comes off, you'll release the nanoparticles and infect anyone within fifty metres who inhales them. Give it to me now and this could all be over."

"I really don't think so," Allegra said. "It's my ticket out of here and Starfish is expecting it."

"It's MI6 agent Nathan Hall, isn't it?" Jessica said tersely. "He's Starfish."

"I don't know his real name and I don't care." Allegra smirked as she carefully put the canister back in her handbag. "We weren't on first-name terms."

"How's that even possible?" Jessica asked.

"Starfish is very private – just like me." She hesitated and glanced over her shoulder. "To be honest, it's been delightfully cloak and dagger. He used a voice disguiser on the phone as well as go-betweens whenever he needed to get a message to me directly. I've never done business like this before."

Which made perfect sense when she was dealing with a spy – or rather, a double agent.

"How did you manage to find Starfish?"

"He found me," Allegra replied. "Somehow, don't ask me how, he knew I'd got Sam and cut me a deal that was too good to turn down. Your father got in the way and made a good fall guy until you interfered."

"Why are you telling her this?" Lyndon appeared by Allegra's side, grimacing.

She jumped a little. "What difference does it make now? We have to get rid of her and her father. Starfish said so. It's part of the deal. We can't go back on it now, *darling*."

"Well, let's get on with it instead of playing your stupid mind games as usual," he said. "I've had enough of them. We're wasting time."

Jessica assessed the burly guards in front of her as the couple bickered. The men were taller and far more muscular than she was. She guessed they pumped iron. They were stronger but she still had the element of surprise on her side.

She lurched forward and brought her elbow up sharply. She struck the first guard under the chin with a resounding crack. He lost his balance and fell back a pace, startled. She advanced and performed a roundhouse kick, followed by one behind his knee. She wasn't as strong or as steady on her feet as usual but she still managed to bring the man to the floor. The second guard lunged at her with a syringe but she knocked it out of his hand. She clasped her hands around his neck and pulled him down towards her. She brought her knee up as hard as she could, landing a blow in his solar plexus. He spluttered for breath but she kicked his feet out from under him.

"Jessica! Watch out!" Sam shouted.

She swung around but wasn't quick enough. Lyndon struck her hard in the stomach, winding her. She fell to her knees, gasping for breath.

"It's time we finally put this stupid girl and her dad out of their misery," he said. "They've plagued us for long enough. Get her up."

He clicked his fingers at the guards who'd managed to recover their breath. They pulled her roughly to her feet and dragged her down the corridor. Allegra swiped open a door, revealing a figure lying curled up in a ball on the floor. He looked like a corpse, with white skin stretched over gaunt, hollow cheekbones. It took her a couple of seconds to recognize her dad. He didn't appear to be breathing. A slight tremor gave her a faint glimmer of hope.

"Dad!"

She struggled with the guards, who pinned her hands tightly behind her back. She longed to throw her arms around him but couldn't break free. Her captors were too strong. Had he been injected with Teenosity as well? Was he going to age before her?

"What have you done to him?" she demanded.

"He's sedated with the same drug as you were,"

Allegra said lightly.

"Do you know what you've done?" she yelled. "You can't give a drug like that to someone with M.S. He may never regain the feeling in his limbs like I did."

"Do you think I care?" Allegra said.

Jessica tried to lunge at her but one of the guards twisted her arm harder. She cried out with pain.

"There, there, calm down," Allegra said. "There's no point getting all het up. It won't help your father."

"Wake up." Lyndon shook him.

He heaved her dad to his feet. His eyes opened briefly. They looked glassy and rolled around in their sockets before closing again. His arms hung limply and his legs couldn't hold his weight.

"Dad! It's me, Jessica!" she shouted. "Wake up!"

His eyes didn't reopen. He was locked in his own faraway world that she couldn't reach. Lyndon heaved both her dad's arms over his shoulders and dragged him out of the room. His head flopped back as if he no longer had any control over it.

"Please do something," she said, turning to Allegra. "I'm begging you. You can't do this. He needs to see a doctor. He's ill."

Allegra ignored her and followed Lyndon. Jessica's mind whirred, trying to figure out what to do. She couldn't make a break for it. Even if she did, she couldn't possibly carry her dad single-handedly. She still felt weak and Sam was unsteady on his feet. He couldn't help. They were at the mercy of Allegra and Lyndon. It was hopeless. They'd already tampered with her phones so she couldn't call for help and there was no sign of the police. Becky couldn't have checked her emails. She might not go online until tonight and by then it would be too late. They'd all be dead.

Lyndon led the group along the corridor. He hoisted her dad over his shoulders as they reached the stairs. Allegra's stilettos clattered as she climbed up after him. They argued in hushed voices while the guards muttered into their walkie-talkies. As they reached the lab, three more guards joined them, armed with machine guns.

"This is where we have to part ways." Allegra pushed Jessica into the clean room.

Lyndon dragged her dad in and backed away. She crouched down beside him. His breathing was shallow and laboured.

"Say your goodbyes to Mr Bishop," Allegra said. "It's the last time you'll ever see him. He's coming with us."

He stumbled as a guard pushed him towards Allegra. He grabbed the work surface, trying to regain his balance.

Jessica rose to her feet. "What are you going to do to him?"

"We're taking him to Starfish, along with the vial of his precious formula, in exchange for fifty million pounds."

"No!" Jessica cried. "Starfish betrayed you. He's going to hand him over to a terrorist. You can't want that to happen."

"Do you mean Vectra? He's my number-one fan." Allegra beamed at them. "Apparently he adores my pioneering work and my vision. He's got great plans for you, Sam. He can't wait to try out your creation on his enemies."

Sam looked appalled. "I won't be a part of this!" He tried to back away but a guard shoved him closer to Allegra, almost sending him sprawling to the floor again.

"That's for you to argue with your new boss, not

me," Allegra said coldly. "I don't care what you want. You're useless to me now."

"You can't let Vectra get his hands on Teenosity!" Jessica exclaimed. "He could mass-produce the nanorobots and release them in shopping malls or football stadiums."

"She's right," Sam said. "If Teenosity gets into an air-conditioning system, it could maim or kill thousands of people."

"That's none of my concern," Allegra snapped.

Sam tried to launch himself at Allegra but he was too slow. Lyndon stepped in and poleaxed him with an elbow to the stomach. His head gave a sickening thud as it hit the ground. He lay motionless. Jessica tried to reach him but a guard shoved her back.

"You'd better not have killed him!" Allegra screeched.

"He's unconscious," Lyndon said, checking Sam's pulse. "Now for God's sake, let's get on with this. We should have blown the labs by now. We're late for the rendezvous point. Starfish will come here looking for us before long."

"Starfish can wait," Allegra said, glowering at him. "I want to enjoy this."

Lyndon glared back. "Well, if you won't give the order, I will."

He clicked his fingers and two guards peeled away to the furthest corner of the lab. They crouched down, their backs turned.

"What are they doing?" Jessica said.

"They're setting timers for the explosives," Allegra replied. "There'll be nothing left of the building when I'm finished with it. I can't risk any evidence being discovered when I've left, including your disfigured bodies. You see, I've planned something special with Starfish and Vectra, just for the two of you."

She pointed at the ceiling of the clean room.

"Look up at the vents above your head, Jessica. Soon, a lethal, aerosolized dose of Teenosity will be blasted out. Within seconds, your body will start decaying from within. You'll age from fourteen to eighty in sixty agonizing seconds. Dying in the blast will be a relief after this."

Jessica stared at her, horrified. She was mad enough to carry out her threats.

"That's right. It's not going to be pretty," Allegra

said. "I imagine it'll be extremely painful but Starfish and Vectra both agreed it would be a useful experiment. Sam was right. Contaminating air-conditioning units must be a natural next step from this. Let's see how Teenosity works airborne, shall we?"

"No! Don't!" a voice said weakly.

"Dad!" She threw her arms around his neck as he struggled to sit up.

"So you're with us after all, Jack," Allegra said.

"Please," he whispered. "Spare my daughter. She doesn't deserve this. Kill me, but let my daughter live."

"No, Dad! I won't leave you."

"How touching," Allegra said. "I'd hate to be the one to separate the two of you. You can die together. But first. . ."

She stepped forward and ripped the emerald ring from Jessica's finger.

"I won't make the same mistake again. Starfish said to look out for this." She examined the ring. Her fingers expertly flicked open the secret catch. A laser shot out and died again as she snapped it shut. She placed the ring on the counter.

"Amazing what MI6 can do nowadays," she said,

"but I'm feeling particularly generous today, so you can have this back, as it's worthless."

She threw an object at her.

"Starfish said it belonged to your mother and you'd want to wear it when you died."

Jessica reached out and caught her mum's necklace. She held it tightly in her fist. She wished she'd grabbed the flamethrower or compact off Nathan and used them on him when she had a chance. Only he could have known how important the pendant was to her. Her mum wore it in the photo he kept in his wallet. He kept trophies too, just like Allegra.

"It's tragic when one loses their mother so young," Allegra said suddenly. "We have more in common than you think."

"I really don't think so," Jessica spat back. "You're certifiable. I'm not."

Allegra shook her head. "I lost my mother when I was four, just like you, and things were never the same again. My stepmother never understood me. She never wanted me to model. She never wanted me."

Her eyes misted up as the guards rejoined her. She ignored Lyndon, who impatiently checked his watch.

"Think of your mother now," Jessica said urgently. "She wouldn't want you to do any of this."

"I tried to tell the voices but they wouldn't listen." Allegra started to sob. "They're too strong."

"What voices?"

"The voices in my head."

Jessica walked towards her. Allegra had lost her mind, but Jessica had found a chink in her madness. If she could get her to talk more about her mum, she might have a chance of getting through to her.

"The voices are talking to me again," Allegra said, a hint of a smile hovering on her glossy, scarlet lips.

"What do they say? Are they telling you to let us go?"

"No. They're saying they've had enough of your delaying tactics."

Allegra hit a button on the wall and the door slid shut, sealing them into the room.

CHAPTER
TWENTY TWO

"Let us out!" Jessica screamed, banging on the glass. "Please!"

"It's no good," her dad said weakly. He pushed himself up into a sitting position. "I'm so sorry you got caught up in all this. It's my fault."

"No, it isn't. We can't give up, Dad. We have to think of something."

"You've got two minutes." Allegra appeared at the window, her voice taunting them over the intercom.

Lyndon's voice rang out. "For God's sake, Allegra, stop messing with them. They're trapped and we've got eight minutes until the whole building blows. We have to get out right now!"

Allegra put her hand on the glass and sighed.

"It genuinely pains me to say goodbye. I'd wanted to see the fear in your eyes, the look of horror on your deformed faces as you prayed for death to come quickly. I'll leave this for you both as a reminder of me."

She propped up a digital timer on the ledge outside the room. It was counting down – one minute, thirty seconds.

"No!"

Jessica banged on the glass as Lyndon threw Sam over his shoulder and steered Allegra out of the room. The guards avoided making eye contact with her as they followed.

"Come back! Help us!"

She looked frantically about. The weak points had to be the glass partition and the doors going in and out of the clean room. She clawed desperately at one door, then the next, but it was no good. They were sealed tightly inside. If only Nathan hadn't tipped off Allegra about her laser ring. She could have used it to cut their way out. She looked up at the vents. Within seconds, they'd be blasted with Teenosity.

"Help me block the vents, Dad," she said. "I need a leg up."

"We don't have time to block them all. Here, use this to cover your mouth and nose."

He tore strips off his shirt and handed them to her. She tied them around her face, knowing it was pointless. The nanoparticles would easily pass through the fabric. She bent over to help her dad tie his strip. Something sharp stabbed her in the stomach. She winced, feeling through her sweater. Her fingers touched something small and hard. It was her diamond belly-button stud. She'd forgotten she was wearing it. More importantly, Starfish had forgotten to tell Allegra she still had it.

"One minute and twenty seconds."

Whipping off the stud, she rotated it until she heard a click. She drew on the glass, all the way around the frame, and waited. Nothing happened. It was supposed to disintegrate on impact, wasn't it? What had Nathan said? If only she'd paid more attention.

Sixty seconds. Fifty-nine, fifty-eight, fifty-seven, fifty-six, fifty-five.

Work, please work. She was about to try again when her dad caught her wrist and pulled her back sharply.

"Wait," he said.

There was a loud crack and a faint line appeared across the glass.

"Is that all it does?" She couldn't believe it. She'd failed. It was over.

Thirty seconds.

The vents hissed ominously overhead.

There was a terrific bang. The glass exploded and shattered outwards. She grabbed her dad's hand and pulled him after her. He summoned up his last shred of strength to hurl himself through the gap as the vents opened and spluttered. She dragged him further away, terrified that nanoparticles would still blast out any second.

"Don't worry," he said. "The room's depressurized so the vents won't work now, but we've got a bigger problem. The building's going to blow. We've probably got about six minutes if Lyndon's countdown was accurate. You have to get out of here now. You have to leave me. I'll hold you up."

"I'm not going without you. You can do this, Dad, I know you can. We're both going to get out of here."

She hauled him to his feet, her knees almost crumpling under his weight. She threw his arm over

282

her good shoulder and pulled him to the door, glass crunching beneath her feet. Something green shone between the shards. She propped her dad up against the wall and reached down to grab her emerald ring. Allegra had left it on the counter and the blast must have knocked it off. Jessica slipped it on her finger. She might need it.

She pushed her dad through the door and they stumbled out into the main corridor. Minutes later the first explosion rocked the lab. She steadied herself against the wall, her ears ringing. Her dad's legs went from under him and he sank to the floor. They both coughed violently as they were engulfed in a cloud of dust.

"I can't do it," he said. "Leave me, Jessica. I'm begging you. Get out."

His voice sounded tinny and a long way away. Her eardrums must have ruptured.

"No!"

She looked up the corridor. Sam was sprawled face down. The guards must have messed up and detonated the explosives early. Lyndon and Allegra hadn't had time to get him out before the building exploded, so they'd abandoned him. They'd probably figured they didn't need him as long as they still had the canister. That was still worth fifty million pounds. Now Jessica and her dad had even less chance to get out alive, but she couldn't give up. She put her arms beneath her dad's armpits and heaved, dragging him a few paces as another explosion hit. A jet of flame shot out of the lab. Acrid smoke billowed down the corridor, scorching her lungs and stinging her eyes. She was thrown to the floor, hitting her head. Her dad landed nearby. She could taste something hot and metallic in her mouth. She touched her lip. It was wet with blood. The floor rocked. She couldn't get up again, let alone move her dad *and* Sam.

Suddenly, she was pulled to her feet. She stared into a familiar face.

"Starfish!" She spat the word out like venom, punching Nathan square in the jaw.

"What?" He looked bewildered.

"You came back for Sam. It's the only way you could have known we were here."

"You're wrong!" Nathan shouted. "Your friend Becky raised the alarm at MI6 HQ in London."

"You're lying! You sent me here to die. You wanted to get rid of me and Dad. Mum was expendable to you too. You betrayed us all."

He grabbed her arm roughly. "I don't have time for your conspiracy theories. We have to get out of here now before we all die."

He pulled her down the corridor, towards her dad, as three armed men wearing breathing apparatuses appeared. One lifted up Sam and another hoisted her dad over his shoulders. She tried to break away as Nathan dragged her towards them.

"Let go of me! I hate you! You tried to kill me."

"Come with us, you idiot," he spat back, "or you'll get us all killed."

The next explosion flung them all to the floor and more debris showered over them. Flames fanned down from the ceiling. She put her sleeve in front of her mouth. It felt as though the oxygen was being sucked out of her lungs. She couldn't breathe. The flames were scorching her clothes and hair.

"We're almost there," Nathan said, panting. He pulled her up again. "Down here!"

They ran down the corridor and turned right. Now

they were in the lobby. The men carrying Sam and her dad were the first to escape through the shattered doors, and Jessica and Nathan followed. The next explosion was even more powerful than all the others. Windows blew from the building and flames spurted out.

"Run!" one of the men shouted.

They dived for cover as shards of glass rained down. Jessica looked up and saw a large piece of burning debris hurtling towards them. She screamed. She felt Nathan's hand on her back. He shoved her. She hit the ground and rolled away in time to see him stumble. He was struck hard and fell, flames licking over his body. Firefighters sprang forward and dragged him to safety. They smothered him in foam before paramedics raced up and started pumping his chest and doing mouth-to-mouth.

She watched in horror. It should have been her. The debris had missed her by a fraction of an inch. He'd saved her life. He must have misjudged it as he pushed her towards the debris. In a split second she'd escaped injury while he was seriously hurt. She reeled backwards as firefighters aimed jets of water at the flames.

She spotted her dad and Sam being stretchered on to nearby ambulances wearing oxygen masks, and staggered towards them. Margaret Becker stood nearby, talking to a group of paramedics. She wore a bright red patterned Liberty scarf that made her face look pale and strained. She gave a curt nod in Jessica's direction and turned away to take a call on her mobile.

"Dad!" She jumped into the ambulance and placed her head on his chest.

He took off his oxygen mask. "Are you OK, jellybean?"

She couldn't stop shaking. "Nathan Hall just tried to kill me."

Her dad attempted to speak but was gripped by a violent coughing fit. A paramedic replaced the mask on his face and checked his pulse. His breathing became more regular.

"I'm fine, Dad. It's you I'm worried about."

She looked over her shoulder as Margaret climbed aboard.

"Thank God you're safe, Jack," she said. "You too, Jessica. I saw what happened back there. You were lucky to survive Nathan's attempt on your life."

Her dad mumbled as he tried to remove the mask again. "I have to—"

A paramedic batted his hand away.

"Your oxygen levels are dangerously low," the man said. "Stop wasting your energy by talking. We need to get you to hospital."

"Don't worry, Dad. We can speak later when you're up to it." Jessica held his hand. She glanced up at Margaret. "You need to stop Allegra Knight. She's launching a cream that's going to maim thousands of teenagers."

"Where is she now?" Margaret demanded.

"There's a press event at the top of the Eiffel Tower at nine a.m. She's doing a live television broadcast to launch Teenosity. I'm supposed to be there."

"Well, we don't want to disappoint her, do we? Are you coming?"

Jessica was torn. She wanted to be with her dad but she had to help stop Allegra.

"We need to leave now," Margaret said. "I can't wait." She climbed out.

Jessica looked down at her dad. He squeezed her hand.

"Are you sure?" she asked.

He nodded.

She planted a quick kiss on his forehead and ran after Margaret. As she caught up, she could hear Margaret barking orders into her mobile, arranging for every bottle of Teenosity to be tracked down across Europe and confiscated. Margaret climbed into a black Merc and flung open the passenger door for Jessica. She stuck a siren on the top of the car, which blared loudly.

"Buckle up," she said, reversing at speed.

Margaret nipped in and out of streets, avoiding traffic and hammering on her horn when motorists ignored her siren. Jessica glanced at the clock on the dashboard. They only had fifteen minutes to stop the launch.

"We're going to make it," Margaret said. "I've sent advance teams already."

Jessica clung on to the door handle as they screeched around a sharp corner. As they approached the Eiffel Tower, she spotted police cordons sealing off the area. A handful of tourists stood behind them, watching the flurry of activity with curiosity. The Merc screeched to a halt.

"Ready?" Margaret said.

She nodded. They jumped out and sprinted to the lifts at the base of the structure, which was guarded by eight gendarmes armed with machine guns. Another six armed officers followed them into the lift. She pressed herself against the side as they soared to the top. She closed her eyes and tried to concentrate on stopping Allegra instead of thinking about how high up they were. She couldn't let her fear of heights paralyse her now.

The lift doors opened with two minutes to spare. They piled out into a throng of photographers and journalists. Allegra stood at a microphone, next to a huge plasma screen at the front. She was immaculate as usual in a blue silk Diane von Furstenberg wrap dress and a long string of pearls. Her trademark sunglasses were firmly in place but her red lipstick was smeared.

"Thank you for joining me on such an important day for the beauty industry," she said. "Today marks the turning point in the development of anti-ageing creams. I give you Teenosity!"

Sleek white bottles of face cream appeared on

the plasma screen next to her as the crowd clapped politely.

"Never again will teenagers have to worry about ageing thanks to a breakthrough in nanotechnology. I'm here to tell you today that I, the world-famous Allegra Knight, have found a cure for ageing. Teenosity stops the deterioration of skin cells in its tracks."

The journalists gasped. A few cheered and clapped.

"My face cream provides hope for the next generation, and I can think of no one better to represent Teenosity than the industry's hottest new model, Jessica Cole," Allegra said.

Jessica's photograph flashed up, showing her soaring gracefully through the air in her sparkling Marc Jacobs gown. It was the shot from the warehouse before the attempt on her life.

"Unfortunately Jessica can't join us today due to her other modelling commitments, but I know she shares my excitement about Teenosity," Allegra said. "This event is being screened in thousands of beauty and clothes stores across Europe. On my word, they will begin selling Teenosity for the first time ever."

Images of beauty counters in different shops

appeared on the screen. Assistants stared expectantly at the camera in front of displays of Teenosity bottles.

"Now, in Jessica's absence, I'd be extremely grateful if you would assist me in counting down to the launch of Teenosity. Ten seconds, nine, eight—"

"Stop!" Jessica pushed her way through the crowd.

CHAPTER
TWENTY THREE

"That looks like Jessica Cole," Trudy Tressler, a famous fashion magazine editor, said loudly. "I thought Allegra said she couldn't make it?"

The guests stared as she made her way to the front, followed by the officers.

"It's over, Allegra," she said firmly. "You're not going ahead with this. MI6 and the police have surrounded you. You need to give yourself up."

Allegra paled. Lyndon stepped forward and whispered something in her ear. She looked exasperated and batted him away.

"I have no idea what you're talking about," she insisted. "The launch is going ahead as planned. Seven seconds, six. . ."

Jessica grabbed the microphone, pushing Allegra out of the way. Allegra's sunglasses flew off, exposing bulging, wild eyes.

"Teenosity is toxic and will maim anyone who uses it. You can't sell it!" Jessica shouted.

"Miss Cole is right," Margaret said, taking the microphone off her. "These creams mustn't be sold. All stores should remove the bottles from the shop floor and make sure the seals on the packaging are kept intact."

Gasps rippled through the crowd and photographers jostled to take Jessica's picture.

"How dare you?" Allegra hissed. She turned to the crowd. "Don't listen to them! This is my life's work. They're trying to ruin me because they're jealous of my success."

"It's over," Jessica repeated.

"No it's not!" Allegra screamed. "It's not over until I say it's over. They have to sell Teenosity. Those girls have to be made to pay."

She reached into her handbag.

"She's still got the canister of Teenosity!" Margaret yelled. "She's going to release it. Take her out!"

An officer dived forward and wrestled Allegra to the ground. Margaret snatched the canister from her fingers and held it up triumphantly.

"I've got it! It's safe."

Two officers pinned down Allegra while another handcuffed Lyndon.

"How dare you! Get your hands off me!" Allegra aimed kicks at the officers with her silver Jimmy Choo stilettos as they tried to handcuff her.

"Do you know who I am?" she screeched. "I'm Allegra Knight, the greatest supermodel in the world! You can't treat me like this!"

The guests looked stunned as she was dragged to the lifts.

"I'm sorry, ladies and gentlemen, but the launch of Teenosity is cancelled," a senior French officer said. "I understand from my British colleagues we have Jessica Cole to thank for averting a major catastrophe."

The journalists surged towards her, barking questions.

"What is Teenosity?"

"What's wrong with it?"

"You need to ask the police," she said politely, "but if you'll excuse me, I want to go and see my dad."

Margaret helped clear a path through the crowd and they finally made it to the lifts. Jessica sank against the wall as the doors closed.

"Do you think Allegra would have released the canister?" she said.

"We'll never know, thankfully," Margaret said, "but this job teaches you to expect the unexpected."

She hesitated as the lift jolted and began its descent.

"I wanted to tell you how sorry I am that I didn't believe you or your dad from the beginning. I was wrong. I should never have listened to Nathan, but he managed to convince us all that your dad was Starfish."

"It was Nathan all along, wasn't it?" Jessica said. "It all made sense when I overheard the telephone conversation in his hotel room and found the photo in his wallet."

Margaret pushed her hair behind her ears. "I'm afraid so. We've discovered he uploaded the file linking your dad to Vectra on his computer and set up a ghost bank account. The five hundred thousand pounds never existed. It appeared in your dad's bank statement but it never actually touched his account."

That was clever – and devious. He'd almost got away with it too.

"Allegra said that Starfish wanted to get rid of me and Dad at the same time. That's why Nathan eventually agreed I should go into AKSC."

"You both got in his way and were expendable," Margaret said. "When he realized MI6 was going to storm the building and his plan was ruined, he came to get you first. He almost killed you back there."

Jessica could still feel Nathan's hand on her back as the debris was about to hit them. She shivered.

"We should have investigated Nathan sooner given his history with your father," Margaret said. "We let you down – *I* let you down – and for that I truly apologize. Mrs T wants to apologize in person too."

"Thank you," Jessica said. "That means a lot, but what will happen now?"

"When Nathan regains consciousness, he'll be interrogated. He betrayed his country, attempted to murder you, and we suspect he was involved in the murder of Lara Hopkins. We can't let him get away with it. He will be prosecuted and brought to justice."

CHAPTER
TWENTY FOUR

Two days later, Jessica perched lightly on the side of the hospital bed, careful not to put pressure on her dad's legs. His eyes remained closed. He'd lost consciousness shortly after arriving at hospital but his condition had stabilized. Although he remained hooked up to a breathing apparatus and a heart monitor, he looked much healthier. His face was pale and gaunt but no longer the terrible near-death grey colour it had been.

"He's strong. He's going to come through this." Mattie squeezed her shoulder. "He'll wake up when he's ready. You'll see.'

"I know." She flashed a smile at her grandma.

Jessica had phoned her after Allegra was arrested

and Mattie had flown in straight away. Considering the pack of lies Jessica had told her over the last few days, she'd taken everything pretty well so far. Admittedly, she'd threatened to ground her until she was, like, eighteen. But she hadn't gone *totally* ballistic, and she was definitely more concerned about how she and her dad were doing.

Mattie sat down next to the bed and removed her navy Chanel jacket. She smiled at Jessica as she reached over and squeezed her dad's hand.

"He'll be so proud of you when he finds out what you did," she said. "Naturally, I'm still furious that you went off behind my back like that, but I'm proud too. Jack wouldn't be here today if it wasn't for you."

"We were both lucky," Jessica said. "But Mum wasn't. I know she used to be an MI6 spy and that she died on the job."

Mattie let out a little cry and dropped her dad's hand. "Who told you?"

"It doesn't matter. The point is, why didn't *you* or Dad tell me?"

"Because telling you wouldn't bring her back," she said, fighting back tears. "We both wanted to give you some sense of normality when your family wasn't normal. It was far from it. We wanted you to have happy memories."

She looked away, refusing to meet Jessica's gaze.

"I do have happy memories, but there's something else you're not telling me." Jessica stood up. "I can sense it. What is it? You think you're protecting me but you're not."

"This last week has shown me that I can't protect you from everything," Mattie said sadly. "However much I may want to."

"So tell me."

Mattie played with the sapphire ring on her index finger. "What I have to say is going to be difficult for you, but I want you to know that things are going to change when we get back home. Jack and I will always be here if you want to talk about Mum. You have my word."

"What is it?" Jessica was suddenly afraid. She wished Dad would wake up right now. He'd call her jellybean before hugging her and making everything feel OK.

Mattie took a deep breath. "The helicopter crash,"

she blurted out. "Your father suspected it wasn't an accident. That's why we never talk about it. We thought it was too much for you to cope with."

Jessica felt the room lurch. "You're saying it was deliberate?"

"We don't know for sure. Accident investigators discovered that the pilot had high levels of barbiturates in his bloodstream. He wasn't fit to fly. It's possible he passed out or fell asleep while in the air."

"So it was his fault?" Her voice sounded distant.

"He didn't have a history of drug abuse," Mattie said. "It's possible his drink was spiked, but your father was never able to prove anything."

Jessica stared at her dad, willing him to regain consciousness.

"He blamed Nathan Hall, didn't he? They fell out about the crash."

Mattie gave her a strange look. "Yes, that's correct."

"So Nathan could have spiked the pilot's drink and made sure he missed the flight. He's held some kind of grudge against our family ever since."

Mattie shook her head. "That can't be true."

"But it is. Don't you see? He's Starfish – a double

agent. He set Dad up because he's done a deal with a terrorist and he tried to kill me."

"He's your godfather, Jessica. He's supposed to protect you."

"What?" She stared at Mattie in disbelief.

"You wouldn't remember him. You haven't seen him since you were very little. He and your father lost touch."

"I don't believe you."

"It's true. That's why Jack made him your contact point in an emergency."

Jessica remembered the photo in his wallet, the way he had reached for her hand to try and comfort her on the Eurostar. She shook off the sentimental images. This made his betrayal far, far worse.

"He pushed me in front of the falling debris."

"Are you sure you weren't mistaken?" Mattie asked. "Couldn't he have tried to save your life? The nurses say he's still in a coma. That could have been you, Jessica."

She glared at Mattie. Why did she always have to contradict her?

"You weren't there. I know what happened and I

know that Dad blamed him for Mum's death, so there's no point trying to hide that from me too."

Mattie bristled. "Yes, I admit he was angry that Nathan hadn't seen the state the pilot was in that day." She folded her arms.

"What else?"

"Your father accused him of being involved in the crash during a row. That's what caused the rift."

"You see! So why are you defending him?"

"Because your father was raw with grief at the time. He lashed out at those closest to him. He didn't know what he was saying. I didn't take his accusations seriously. No one did."

"I think he knew exactly what he was saying." Jessica touched her dad's arm. "He believed Nathan was rotten and so do I. So does MI6. They have proof that he's Starfish."

"What proof? What exactly do they say he's done?"

Jessica tapped her foot impatiently. "I can ask MI6 to give you a full debriefing if you want since you obviously don't believe a word I'm telling you."

"I didn't say that."

Jessica glared at her. "You didn't have to. It's

written all over your face. You'd rather believe a double-crossing murderer instead of me and Dad."

"For goodness' sake, Jessica, stop being so melodramatic! I'm just saying—"

"He's a traitor, you hear me? He betrayed Mum, he betrayed Dad and he betrayed me!"

Jessica stormed out of the room. She took it back about Mattie being reasonable over everything that had happened. Why wouldn't she ever listen to her? She turned the corner, colliding with a cleaner in pink overalls, who was pushing a trolley piled with rags and disinfectant.

"*Pardonnez-moi,*" Jessica said, manoeuvring past.

She strode up the corridor. She wished Dad would wake up – Nathan too, so she could get him to confess. Maybe then Mattie would believe her. There'd be no chance of getting any more info out of Allegra. According to Margaret, she was in a nearby psychiatric hospital and completely gaga, while Lyndon and the security guards were refusing to cooperate with police.

Jessica stopped as she approached the nurses' desk.

"Ohmigod!"

The dark-haired woman looked up, frowning. "What is it?" she said in French.

"Something's wrong!'

Jessica ran back. She'd caught a glimpse of the cleaner's shoes as she bumped into her. They were shiny black-patent courts, not the type of shoes you'd expect a cleaner to wear.

She burst through the door to her dad's private room in time to see Mattie grappling with a syringe in Allegra's hand. Her grandma managed to knee Allegra in the stomach and land a punch on her cheek. Allegra swung back, slamming Mattie against the wall. She crumpled to the floor.

Allegra looked up. "You!" Rage bubbled in her chest like tuberculosis. She leapt to the bedside, pointing the syringe.

"No!" Jessica yelled. "Get off my dad!"

She threw herself across the room at Allegra, knocking the syringe out of her hand. Allegra's fist smacked hard into her stomach. She was surprisingly strong for her tiny frame. Jessica fell to the ground, gasping. Allegra leapt over her, catlike, and was out of the door. Jessica willed herself to ignore the pain and crawled towards Mattie as a nurse burst through the door, red-faced and out of breath.

"What's happened?" the woman demanded.

"Get security," Jessica panted. "We've been attacked."

The nurse hit an alarm button on the wall and dashed out.

Jessica studied Mattie's face anxiously. "Are you OK?"

"I'm fine. She didn't manage to inject me." She winced as she eased herself up the wall.

"I'm sorry, Mattie. For everything." Jessica kissed her forehead as a doctor ran in, followed by another nurse. "I'll be back soon, I promise."

"Wait! Stop!" Mattie tried to grab her hand but she was too quick.

She bolted out of the door and looked up and down the corridor. Nurses ran towards her from the corridor on the right as an alarm sounded. They'd have seen Allegra tear past if she'd gone that way. Jessica turned left, out of the ward and towards the main staircase. She leant over the side, looking up and down, but couldn't see a flash of pink overalls.

She doubled back along the corridor and spotted a fire escape. She darted through the door. Allegra's pink overalls were halfway down the stairs, discarded as she fled to ground level. Then Jessica remembered the games Allegra liked to play. She couldn't fool her this time.

She climbed up the staircase, taking three steps at a time. She burst through the door at the top and emerged on the roof. The cold air was like a slap to her face. Allegra stood on the edge, her dishevelled hair blowing in the wind and her arms outstretched as if she were about to jump.

"No!" Jessica shouted.

Allegra rocked on her feet. She let out a long, hard laugh.

"You've always had it in for me, haven't you, Valerie?" she said. "From the first time we met I could tell you were jealous of the attention Daddy gave me. You wanted him all to yourself and when you realized he loved me more, you punished me day after day."

She was hallucinating. Allegra thought she was her dead stepmother.

"I'm not Valerie, I'm Jessica," she said. "You need

to move away from the edge."

"I don't have to do what you tell me. I don't live in your house any more, remember?"

She turned around, her eyes bright with rage.

"I can help you but you need to give yourself up," Jessica said. "You need proper medical treatment. You need to go back to hospital."

She was close enough to reach out and grab her if she tried to throw herself off the building.

"You'd like that, wouldn't you, Valerie?" Allegra spat back. "You want me locked up for the rest of my life so I can't outshine you any more. You want to destroy my modelling career, but you won't. I'll destroy you first."

She looked strangely at Jessica.

"But I did destroy you, didn't I? You didn't see me behind you until it was too late. I watched you fall, step by step. I listened to the snap of your neck. I watched the life drain out of you and I enjoyed every minute of it."

Ohmigod. Jessica remembered the newspaper cutting she'd found about Valerie Knight's fatal accident. Allegra had killed her own stepmother.

"I'm not your stepmother," she said.

"The voices say you're a liar. You'll be telling me next that security guards are on their way to take me back to the psych ward."

"They are," Jessica said, bluffing. "They'll be here any minute. I told them I was heading up here."

"Really? Then what are they doing down there?" Allegra peered over the edge and pointed to the ground. "They're sealing off the main staircases and the exits. No one knows you're up here, Jessica, except me."

CHAPTER
TWENTY FIVE

Jessica took a step back, realizing her catastrophic mistake, but Allegra's long, sharp talons had already encircled her wrist. She yanked her forward, trapping her in a tight neck lock. Jessica lost her balance and the car park lurched towards her. She opened her mouth but all that came out was a silent, inward scream. She was gripped by an overwhelming desire to see her dad one last time.

"It's a long way down, isn't it?" Allegra laughed in her ear. "I liked the vision about my stepmother, didn't you? I thought that was a particularly nice touch, along with the voices in my head telling me to do bad things. Psychiatrists love all that stuff. They lapped it up in hospital, the same way you did in the lab. The morons thought they could cure me with a cocktail of drugs. Still, it was so much better than prison. That would have been far harder to break out of."

"So you made everything up?

"Oh no, not everything. I did murder my stepmother. She deserved it. Now I'm going to murder you. I think I'll enjoy it almost as much."

"You're insane!"

Jessica tried to regain her balance, but Allegra's arm was tight around her neck. She couldn't risk trying to disentangle herself. One wrong move and they'd both fly over the edge. She had to stall for time. It was her only hope.

"How did you escape from the hospital?" she gasped, struggling to breathe as Allegra's arm crushed her windpipe.

"It was surprisingly easy," Allegra admitted. "I stole a doctor's key card and helped myself to a syringe and drugs from the pharmacy. I took some clothes and money and smuggled myself out among the dirty laundry. It wasn't terribly pleasant, but one thing kept me going. Do you know what that was?"

Her grip tightened even further. Jessica clawed desperately at her arm but it remained locked in a death grip.

"It was revenge," Allegra hissed. "You and your father destroyed everything I'd been working for. I had to watch *my* dream, *my* Teenosity, being snatched away from me by a freckle-faced muppet and a cripple. I had to find you both and I knew this was the only hospital your father could be brought to in his condition. Now it's payback time. Do you have any last requests before you die?"

"Just . . . just . . . one. . . What did Starfish tell you about my mum?"

The question caught Allegra by surprise. She loosened her grip. Her feet rocked and they both almost tumbled over the edge.

"What do you mean?"

"Starfish told you to give me my mum's necklace before I died and I know you were taunting me with the flowers in my room. Only Starfish could have told you my mum's name was Lily and her favourite flowers were roses. It had to be someone close to Mum."

"It always comes back to our mothers, doesn't it?" Allegra let out a sigh. "We both miss them so much, it's like a physical wound that never heals. I think about mine every day."

She paused.

"I guess it doesn't matter now. Starfish told me to kill you because you were sticking your nose into things that didn't concern you. *Like mother, like daughter. They're both better off dead.* Those were Starfish's exact words."

Rage gripped Jessica, sending adrenaline pumping through her body. She tried to tug Allegra's arm away from her neck but it was rigid and immovable. She felt the emerald ring on her index finger swivel beneath the force of her grip and dig into Allegra's arm.

"Don't worry," Allegra said, peering over the side of the building. "I'll be sure to send a gorgeous wreath and commiserations card to your father from somewhere nice and sunny. He's going to be devastated. Losing a wife is bad enough, but a daughter as well. Tut, tut, tut. Now that's just careless."

Jessica let go of Allegra's arm as she was about

to swing her over the edge. She snapped back the gemstone setting and a laser bored into Allegra's cheek, filling the air with the smell of burning flesh.

"Aaaaargh!" Allegra's shriek was high-pitched and animal-like.

Jessica ducked beneath her arm as Allegra staggered backwards and toppled over the edge. Jessica tried to grab her but she slipped, screaming, between her fingers. Jessica sank to the ground, shell-shocked. She couldn't bear to watch the impact. It felt like minutes but could only have been a few seconds. Next, she heard shouts from the ground below, then cheers and people clapping.

Sick or what?

What kind of weirdoes applauded when someone fell to their death? She peered over the edge just in time to see Allegra scrambling to her feet.

What the—? It was impossible. She couldn't possibly have survived a fall like that.

"Stop her!" Jessica yelled.

She leant over the edge and watched, flabbergasted, as Allegra limped over to a taxi rank. She looked back and waved at Jessica before climbing inside a cab. It pulled away, mingling with the traffic before turning the corner and disappearing.

No way!

Jessica pulled herself up and found her hand tangled in something. She looked closer. A thin, barely visible piece of thread was anchored to a hook at the edge of the roof. It billowed in the wind, stretching down the side of the building. It was the same nano thread that had saved her life in the warehouse.

Allegra must have smuggled some into the psychiatric hospital and attached herself to the side of this building. She'd wanted them both to fall, knowing that only she would survive.

Jessica closed her eyes and inhaled deeply as she touched her mum's pendant. She could have sworn she just caught a whiff of roses from the air-conditioning unit nearby. Now she had a new childhood memory: a nursery rhyme her mum used to recite to her when she was tucked up in bed.

Run, run as fast as you can.

You can't catch me, I'm the gingerbread man.

Allegra could run but Jessica would catch her eventually. She swore on her mum's necklace, she would.

Two Weeks Later

Jessica whipped a dish of vegetarian lasagne out of the oven. She carried it into the dining room, careful not to drip melted cheese on to her latest find from Portobello Market: a peppermint chiffon vintage Chanel prom dress. Salads, quiches and cakes covered the table, but she managed to make room for the dish. Mattie had really gone to town on the catering.

Her dad's welcome home from hospital party was in full swing. Guests milled about, chatting and eating. All this seemed worlds away from what had been going on. Jessica half-expected Allegra or Vectra to leap out at her; they were both still at large. Vectra had managed to evade capture in Paris despite being surrounded by police in a warehouse. He was suspected of murdering MI6 agent Lara Hopkins and many more people.

She was safe for now, and her dad said she had to concentrate on all the positives instead. They were together again, and she'd grown closer to Mattie, something she wouldn't have thought possible a few months ago. She'd saved thousands of teenage girls from being maimed, and every bottle of Teenosity had been destroyed at a secure government facility.

Then there was her PFB. Potential Future Boyfriend. Fingers crossed. Everything crossed.

She and Jamie had been texting each other a lot recently and she'd invited him to the party. They hadn't had a chance to talk yet. He was in the corner of the room, chatting to Becky and Sam Bishop – except that wasn't his name any more. He was Tony Harper, retired chemist. She felt butterflies in her stomach as she watched Jamie. He was truly drop-dead gorgeous.

Becky and Jamie thought they were talking to a pensioner. They had no idea who Sam really was; MI6 had forced him to sign the Official Secrets Act and take on a new identity. There was a risk that Vectra could come after him again. His condition was stable, but no antidote existed to reverse the damage. He'd vowed to continue with his research to find his own cure. She was sure he'd find it one day, but nobody knew whether it would come soon enough to help Tyler and the other maimed supermodels. They'd all had plastic surgery to try and repair their aged faces, with little success.

Tyler was the only one to go public about her ordeal so far and had sold her story to *OK!* for a million pounds. She released a photo of herself before she'd undergone plastic surgery. She looked like a fifty-year-old, not eighteen. She had crow's feet around her eyes and deep furrows on her forehead and cheeks. Her chest was wrinkly too. She blamed her dramatic ageing on a fashion shoot at a nuclear plant last year. She was suing the plant, the clothing company and Emerald as well, campaigning for safer disposal of nuclear waste. MI6 had gone into damage limitation mode and never told her or the other supermodels that they'd actually been mutilated by Allegra at the Emerald ball.

Jessica looked around the room. Government spooks, pretending to be from the Foreign Office, mingled with models and her school friends. If Becky realized who some of these people were she'd probably hyperventilate. Margaret waved at her. She was wearing a shocking pink Liberty scarf today. She looked happy and relaxed as her two grandchildren scampered about, playing peekaboo.

Jessica couldn't see Dad anywhere. He never felt

comfortable at parties. Where was he hiding? She ducked out of the room and went to the study.

"There you are," she said, peeking around the door. "Your guests will start to wonder where you are."

Her dad rolled his wheelchair around the desk. He hadn't been able to walk unaided since Allegra's injection. His face was pale and he looked as though he'd been crying.

"That was Mrs T on the phone." He picked up the picture of her mum from his desk. "Nathan's been transferred to a London hospital that specializes in coma patients."

Jessica closed the door behind her. "You're upset. I get that. We may never get to hear Nathan's explanation. I want to hear why he did it too."

Her dad shook his head. "It's not that. I never got to say sorry."

"What?" Jessica stared at him, stunned. It was the last thing she expected him to say.

"I'm sorry for accusing him of being involved in Mum's death. It's something I've always regretted."

She paused as the news sunk in. "You don't believe he was involved any more?"

"I never believed it at the time. I said it in the heat of the moment because I wanted to hurt him, to hurt someone for what happened to Lily. I was too proud to apologize. It's too late now."

Seriously? This was *unbelievable* after everything that had happened. Allegra had clearly implicated Starfish in her mum's death in their showdown on the hospital rooftop. Why were her dad and Mattie *still* defending Nathan? They seemed blinded by memories from the past. It was a good job *she* could still think rationally.

"I think your instincts were right," Jessica insisted. "MI6 has a stack of evidence that proves he's Starfish. I've read Margaret's witness account of what happened outside the AKSC building. She definitely thinks Nathan attempted to murder me. I believe that too."

Her dad stared into space. "I guess I remember how he used to dote on you when you were little. He was very protective. We fell out but I still trusted him enough to be your Code Red contact. Obviously, I believe you if you think he was trying to kill you. I must have been wrong all this time. I've been wrong about a lot of things. Things I've kept from you, which I shouldn't have."

His eyes watered again as he stared down at her mum's photo.

"Dad?"

"She was about your age when she started, you know. Mattie too."

"Modelling? I know. That's something you *did* tell me."

"No, I mean spying."

Jessica gaped at him. "What? You're kidding."

"Mattie and your mum both started modelling and spying when they were teenagers. They were very much like you – inquisitive and determined."

"No way!" Mattie was the last person she'd suspect of being a spy. She liked Chanel suits, crossword puzzles, fine wine and arguing with her. Then again, it wasn't just her tongue that was super sharp. Her brain was too. Plus she'd managed to fight off Allegra in the hospital. She'd thrown pretty good moves for someone whose hobbies involved yoga and ballroom dancing.

"Is that why Mattie never wanted me to get involved in your work? She didn't want me to become a spy like her and Mum?"

"She was worried you'd join Westwood too."

"Er. What's that?"

"A division of MI6 that recruits models. It also has photographers, designers, stylists – people who travel and have unlimited access to VIP areas in many countries around the world."

Jessica flopped down behind his desk. "You're having a laugh, right?"

"It sounds strange, I know, but models are ideally placed to assist MI6," her dad continued. "They travel the world and mix with rich, powerful people. Sometimes MI6 only finds out that an arms dealer's in town when his girlfriend appears on the front row of a catwalk show. Other times, it's discovered a foreign diplomat is money laundering after his wife splashes out hundreds of thousands of pounds on couture – far more than she could possibly have in her bank account. The information fed back is invaluable."

"Why are you telling me all this? Why now?"

"You said you didn't want any more secrets; that we all needed to be more honest with each other. I don't want to keep things from you any more. I also wanted you to know all the facts before you make a decision."

"About joining Westwood? Are you serious?"

"Mrs T extended the invitation on the phone just now. She was very impressed with the way you handled yourself in Paris. So was I."

Jessica was too shocked to think straight. Her brain was still digesting everything. "Should I do it? What do you think?"

"I think that spying's a risky business, but you know that already. Like Mattie, I want to protect you. But I also know that I can't stand in the way of who you are. What you have the potential to become."

"I don't know what to say."

There was a knock at the door.

Her dad smiled. "You don't have to say anything yet. Think it over."

Margaret peeped around the door. "There you both are. It's time for the dreaded speeches." She winked at Jessica. "I'll try not to embarrass you both too much."

She vanished again, whistling softly.

"Let's talk it over some more later," her dad said quietly. "In the meantime, don't discuss it with your friends. It has to be kept confidential, for obvious reasons."

"OK."

She felt slightly dazed as she followed him into the living room. She immediately spotted Mattie, locked in conversation with Sara and Camille, her Paris chaperone, in the corner. Now she knew for sure that Sara was a spy, but was Camille one too? They could both be members of Westwood. Were they exchanging spy stories with Mattie? She could never think of Mattie in the same way again. She looked about. The models were MI6 agents, and the young men in the corner who claimed they worked in IT at the Foreign Office were spooks too. Was anyone in the room who they seemed?

Margaret picked up a champagne flute and tapped it with a knife.

"Can I have everyone's attention for a minute, please?"

The hum of voices quietened.

A hand touched her back. She shivered slightly. It was Jamie.

"Are you OK?" he asked.

"I am now," she said, smiling.

Jamie was one of the few people in the room who

didn't have a double identity, apart from classmate/ gorgeous god of love, of course. That was Becky's nickname for him, anyway. He'd die if he knew.

"I wanted to thank everyone for coming here today to welcome Jack home from hospital," Margaret said. "No doubt some of you know Jack and I have had a chequered past. We haven't always seen eye to eye, but that's behind us now. I speak for everyone from the Foreign Office here today when I say we're incredibly grateful for the work he's done. I can reveal that thanks to him, a terrorist attack has been successfully averted."

Her dad grinned as the guests toasted him with champagne. Someone called out: "Well done, Jack."

"Of course, I also have to mention his daughter, Jessica, at this point," she said. "Please refill your glasses and toast Jessica, for her bravery and loyalty, not only to her family but also to her country."

A lump came to Jessica's throat as the guests lifted their glasses.

"Cheers!"

"Speech, speech," voices chimed.

Jessica shook her head, blushing furiously.

"No, honestly, I couldn't," she said.

"Oh yes you could!" Jamie laughed and pushed her forward.

"Go, girl!" Becky shouted. She wolf-whistled loudly.

"We won't take no for an answer," Mattie insisted.

"Come on, Jessica!" Sara shouted. "Don't be shy."

"No, really."

"You're too modest," her dad said, smiling.

"Like mother, like daughter," Margaret said. She raised her glass of champagne.

Jessica froze. It felt as if she'd been punched in the stomach.

"Are you all right, Jess?" Jamie asked.

She looked around the room. All eyes were fixed on her. Mattie, Becky and her dad looked puzzled while Margaret gave a hard, unflinching stare. Jessica felt the blood rush to her ears, making a buzzing sound.

"I'll be back in a minute," she said.

She dived out of the room, Allegra's voice ringing in her head.

Like mother, like daughter.

They're both better off dead.

Those were Starfish's exact words.

She didn't believe in coincidences. She suddenly remembered what Margaret had said at the top the Eiffel Tower that day.

She's still got the canister of Teenosity. She's going to release it.

Nobody had told Margaret about the canister. The only way she could have known was if she'd been expecting Allegra to deliver it to her. Allegra was running late and hadn't made it to the rendezvous point with Starfish. She'd gone straight to the Eiffel Tower in time for the launch of Teenosity instead, but Margaret didn't know that.

She gripped the table as another wave of nausea hit her.

Margaret was Starfish, not Nathan.

Margaret had set up Dad and attacked Jessica with chloroform when she disturbed her uploading the file on to his computer. She'd contacted Allegra using a voice disguiser, which made her sound male. She'd cleverly planted the seed of doubt in her head at dinner that night in Paris, that Nathan was working against her dad and that he had something to hide. Margaret had framed him and Jessica had believed every word she'd said. In the meantime, she'd tried to kill Jessica: instructing Allegra and Lyndon to poison the dress, cut the wire on the modelling shoot and finally to test the aerosolized Teenosity on her and Dad.

Unfortunately, Nathan had been right about *her* too. She was headstrong and she'd jumped to conclusions too quickly. She replayed Nathan's telephone conversation in The Ritz in her head again.

So Lily and Jack were expendable and now Jessica is? Right?

If only she'd paid closer attention. It was a question, not a statement. He was challenging Mrs T about sending her into AKSC. He'd pushed her out of the way of the debris, rather than into its path, because he was her godfather. He was trying to protect her. It's what he'd been doing all along when he tried to stop her from going to Paris and getting inside AKSC.

Ohmigod, ohmigod, ohmigod. What had she done?

She'd made it so easy for Margaret. She'd helped her get away with it. Now she had no proof. It was the word of a respected MI6 agent against hers. By now, Margaret would have destroyed any evidence that could possibly lead back to her and planted it all on Nathan. She'd already made sure the ghost bank account was traced to his computer. Then she'd given her witness statement, saying he'd tried to kill her outside the AKSC building. No one knew if Nathan would come out of his coma. It was possible he'd never get the chance to clear his name, thanks to her.

She jumped as someone touched her arm.

"Whoa, steady on. Is everything all right? You looked like you'd seen a ghost back there." Her dad wheeled in front of her.

"Yeah, something like that."

"What is it?"

She raised her chin. "I want you to accept Mrs T's offer. I want to join Westwood."

"You're sure that's what you really want?"

"I've never been more certain of anything in my life. I have to do this. For me. For Mum."

Margaret had better watch out. She was coming for her and Allegra. This time she'd have MI6's resources behind her.

"I can ring Mrs T now if you want," her dad said.

"First I need to go back in there and propose a toast."

He raised an eyebrow. "Really? What to?"

"To unfinished business," Jessica said, reaching for his hand.